THE THORNTHWAITE INHERITANCE

By the same author

THE THORNTHWAITE INHERITANCE

GARETH P. JONES

BLOOMSBURY

LONDON BERLIN NEW YORK SYDNEY

Bloomsbury Publishing, London, Berlin and New York

First published in Great Britain in 2009 by Bloomsbury Publishing Plc
36 Soho Square, London, W1D 3QY

Text copyright © Gareth Jones 2009
The moral right of the author has been asserted

All rights reserved
No part of this publication may be reproduced or
transmitted by any means, electronic, mechanical, photocopying
or otherwise, without the prior permission of the publisher

A CIP catalogue record of this book is available from
the British Library

ISBN 978 0 7475 9982 1

FSC
www.fsc.org
MIX
Paper from
responsible sources
FSC® C018072

BAINTE DEN STOC

WITHDRAWN FROM
DÚN LAOGHAIRE-RATHDOWN COUNTY
LIBRARY STOCK

Typeset by Dorchester Typesetting Group Ltd
Printed in Great Britain by Clays Ltd, St Ives Plc

10

www.bloomsbury.com

For Alex, Molly, Archie and Esme

Leabharlanna Dhún Laoghaire · Ráth An Dúin

ACT ONE

THE TRUCE

Lorelli and Ovid Thornthwaite had been trying to kill each other for so long that neither twin could remember which act of attempted murder came first. Was it Lorelli's cunning scheme to put on a play about the French Revolution, casting Ovid in the role of an aristocrat to be executed using a working guillotine? Or could it have been that long hot summer when Ovid managed to produce an ice lolly containing a small but deadly explosive, triggered by the surrounding ice reaching melting point?

Whoever had struck first, trying to take each other's life was now simply something the Thornthwaite twins did, in the same way that other brothers and sisters might play together, enjoy watching cartoons or squabble over the remote control. Except that compared to playing, watching cartoons or squabbling, trying to kill your twin is much harder work, not to mention illegal, which was why on their thirteenth birthday, having clocked up over two hundred murder attempts between them, Ovid suggested they call a truce.

'I no longer want to kill you,' he announced, his bottle-green eyes meeting his sister's across the table. Two slices of birthday cake sat in front of them. Neither had been touched.

'I have never wanted to kill you,' replied Lorelli, 'I have only ever acted out of self-defence.'

Ovid smiled. 'Whereas self-preservation has always been my motivation,' he said, 'and, as you were the last one to attack, I propose we call it quits.'

'I wasn't the last one to attack,' stated Lorelli, pushing her straight black hair from her face.

'What about the flesh-eating piranha in my bath?'

'That was on Sunday. You booby-trapped my bed on Monday.'

'I'd been working on that for months. I couldn't let all that planning go to waste.' Ovid remembered with pride how he had set up a device in his sister's bedroom that was designed to fling the first thing to sit on the bed out of the window. Lorelli's bedroom was at the top of the central spire of Thornthwaite Manor.

'Poor Cowell had the fright of her life,' said Lorelli.

Ovid had forgotten that the cat liked to jump on her bed for a snooze sometimes.

'Cats have nine lives,' he said. 'We only have one. It

doesn't matter who started it if we both agree to stop now.'

Lorelli eyed him suspiciously. She didn't trust her brother for one second. He had tried this tactic before, waiting for her to lower her guard before unleashing the next lethal scheme.

'I mean it this time,' he said, wearing an expression of deepest sincerity.

'OK,' she said finally, deciding she would go along with the ceasefire while remaining sensibly cautious. 'Truce.'

'Truce,' repeated her brother, grinning.

They leant forward and shook on it before sealing the deal with two slices of birthday cake, which they switched fourteen times before eating, ensuring that neither piece had been tampered with.

THE SUDDEN DEATHS OF LORD &
LADY THORNTHWAITE

The twins' truce came thirteen years after the untimely demise of both their parents. When they were old enough to understand, it was the head servant, Mr Crutcher, who had explained to Lorelli and Ovid the circumstances surrounding the deaths.

Lord Mycroft Thornthwaite had died first very suddenly one Tuesday night after a sumptuous four-course meal with his wife, Lady Martha Thornthwaite, the twins' mother.

The investigating officer was DI Lionel Skinner, who, having spent his career failing to get a promotion in the big city had recently moved to Hexford County Police in order to become a detective inspector. Following the discovery of a slice of melon meringue wedged in the corpse's throat, Skinner concluded that Lord Thornthwaite had choked to death.

Lady Thornthwaite's story supported this conclusion. She claimed to have left the room during dessert to visit the lavatory only to find, upon her return, her husband dead. She said she had heard him coughing from the hallway but assumed that he must have lit one of his stinky cigars. They always made him cough, she said. She had no idea he was choking to death.

'I loved my husband, Inspector Skinner,' she said. 'I can't believe he's gone.'

The story seemed perfectly plausible until the blood tests came back from the post-mortem of the dead body, finding poison in his bloodstream. Further tests revealed traces of the same poison on the dirty dishes upon which the caviar had been served as a starter.

After questioning all the staff, Inspector Skinner learnt that Lady Thornthwaite had given them all the night off, even Mrs Bagshaw, the cook, saying she wanted to prepare the meal herself. When asked by the detective, Mr Crutcher was forced to admit that she had access to all the ingredients that made up the poison that had killed Lord Thornthwaite.

'Why did our mother kill our father?' Lorelli and Ovid had wanted to know.

'Greed can make people do terrible things,' Mr Crutcher had replied before continuing with his story.

It was a wild winter's evening when Mr Crutcher answered the door to DI Skinner and led him to the great hall, where Lady Thornthwaite was waiting, looking every bit the beautiful widow, draped entirely in black.

'Would you care for a sherry, Inspector?' she asked.

'No thank you, ma'am,' he replied.

'You don't mind if I do, do you?' she said, pouring herself a glass of sweet sherry from the decanter.

'Not at all, but I'm sorry to say this is not a social visit.'

Watching her take a sip from the glass, Skinner blurted out, 'I have evidence to suggest that you murdered your husband.'

Before Lady Thornthwaite could respond the phone began to ring.

'I'm sorry, Inspector, do you mind if I get that?' she said.

Outside, the rain pounded on the long windows. Forks of lightning cut across the dark grey sky and thunder growled ominously, growing nearer each time.

Looking back on it, Mr Crutcher would reflect how Lady Thornthwaite had no idea she was about to utter her last words, or else she might have said something more profound. As it was, the last thing Lady Thornthwaite ever said was, 'I simply can't stand to leave a ringing phone unanswered.'

'I know exactly what you mean,' said Inspector Skinner, noting how calm she was for someone who had just been accused of murdering her husband.

She placed her glass of sherry on the mantelshelf above the fireplace and stooped to pick up the earpiece of the old-fashioned phone.

A clap of thunder sounded above, shaking the old manor to its foundations. The room went bright white as lightning struck, creating an image of Lady Thornthwaite that would haunt Inspector Skinner for the rest of his life, burnt into his mind like an over-developed photograph.

Immediately afterwards the power went dead and the room was thrown into darkness.

'Don't be alarmed, ma'am,' said the inspector. 'I carry a torch for just such occasions.'

He pulled a torch from his belt, switched it on and pointed it to where Lady Thornthwaite had been standing.

She wasn't there.

He lowered the beam of light and discovered her lying on the ground, dead, still clutching the telephone earpiece.

This time the forensic tests were conclusive. The twins' mother was killed by a bolt of lightning striking the telephone mast outside, sending one billion volts through the wire, frying the telephone and cooking Lady Thornthwaite's insides.

Inspector Skinner checked the phone records and found that the person who made the call had been trying to get through to his wife to warn her about the storm. He hadn't even known the Thornthwaites.

In other words, Lady Thornthwaite was killed by a wrong number.

THE WILL

The tragic deaths of Lord and Lady Thornthwaite were felt heavily in Thornthwaite Manor. Mr Crutcher decreed that as a sign of respect, only black would be worn and the only music played would be sombre. He commanded Mrs Bagshaw only to cook bland food and he ensured that no light bulb was brighter than 40 watts in order to create a suitably respectful atmosphere. He disconnected the phone and sold the television set so that the household could be pure in its grief, without intrusion from the outside world. The flag, which flew on a flagpole at the highest point of Thornthwaite Manor, above Lorelli's bedroom, was lowered to half mast.

Thirteen years later little had changed. Without television programmes or computer games the twins made do with long games of chess and the books in the library for entertainment. In fact the only change was that, after a prolonged campaign by Mrs Bagshaw,

60-watt bulbs were allowed in the kitchen, where good lighting was required for food preparation.

The twins had grown up in the dark, eating flavourless food, with Ovid playing music in minor keys on the grand piano in the drawing room.

An old family superstition held that it was bad luck for a Thornthwaite to have their photo taken, so the only picture the twins had of their parents was the painting that hung above the fireplace among the other portraits of their ancestors. When the other wasn't looking, each twin would enter the portrait room and sit staring at the painting, searching their mother's face as though it might reveal why she had killed their father.

For centuries each generation had produced only one child, always a boy, all sporting identical jet-black hair and bottle-green eyes, so when Lord Mycroft Thornthwaite, the twins' father, heard Nurse Griddle shout, 'It's a boy,' he had smiled and Mr Crutcher lit his standard celebratory cigar. But before Lord Thornthwaite could take the heavy smoke into his mouth, the nurse cried, 'And a girl!'

Lorelli was the first girl to inherit the distinctive Thornthwaite look, and while all the men, including Ovid, had been cursed with a somewhat startling appearance, his sister was undeniably beautiful.

Ovid finished off his slice of Mrs Bagshaw's 'one spoon' cake, named after the single teaspoon of sugar used to make it, and smiled. 'To a new era of peace and harmony,' he said, raising a glass of bitter lemonade. 'And to the Easter holidays. Two weeks without lessons.'

Although the twins didn't attend school, their teachers, Mr Crutcher and Nurse Griddle, maintained the same school terms and holidays as the outside world.

'I'd like to make it formal this time,' said Lorelli.

'What do you mean by formal?' Ovid replied.

'Put it in the will. So if either of us dies before the age of sixteen the other forfeits their half of the inheritance. That way neither of us has anything to gain from the other's death.'

The late Lord Thornthwaite's will stated that in the event of his and his wife's death the entire fortune be split equally between his two children on their sixteenth birthday. Prior to that, the estate was left under the guardianship of his most trusted employee, Mr Crutcher.

'Who would the inheritance go to if forfeited?' said Ovid.

'Who cares? It can stay in Alfred's hands,' replied Lorelli. 'The point is that, neither of us will get it.'

Ovid paused before looking Lorelli directly in the eyes and replying, 'My dear sister, can't we trust one another?'

'I'd like something in writing this time,' she said simply.

Mr Crutcher, who was standing in the corner of the room waiting on them, stepped forward. 'I can have the family lawyer come round tomorrow and draw up a legal document.'

'I didn't know we had a lawyer,' said Lorelli.

'Oh yes. Mr Farthing,' said Mr Crutcher.

Ovid turned to Lorelli and said, 'Do we really want to get lawyers involved?'

'I'll trust you once I can read it in black and white,' replied Lorelli.

The twins were both bright from an early age but while Ovid favoured maths, history and the sciences taught by Mr Crutcher, Lorelli's heart lay with literature, art and languages, taught by Nurse Griddle. In short, Lorelli believed in things that were written down.

'All right, if it will make you happy, we'll call the lawyer,' relented Ovid.

'Then it's settled,' said Mr Crutcher. 'I'll contact Mr Farthing immediately.'

For Lorelli and Ovid, Thornthwaite Manor had been a dangerous place to grow up in. The twins had come away remarkably unscathed from all the electrocutions, explosions, fires, flying kitchen knives, and even the occasional gun shot. Now, finally, they could put it all behind them.

THE LAWYER

Mr Farthing, the family lawyer, was a small man in every way other than his size; he had a quiet voice, an unassuming manner and a nervous disposition, and he towered above everyone he met. His large facial features were emphasised by a small pair of round spectacles resting on his huge nose. His faded grey suit was several sizes too small for him, the cuffs barely reaching his wrists, the trousers revealing his mismatched socks. All in all he looked like someone who had woken up that morning to discover that he had suddenly grown tall and was still getting used to it.

Mr Crutcher opened the door to Mr Farthing, took his coat and led him through the hall.

'It's been a long time since your last visit, Bernard,' said the head servant.

'Thirteen years,' mumbled Mr Farthing, looking around at the gloomy hallway. 'I last came here after

Lord and Lady Thornthwaite passed away. My dear wife had her ... accident shortly after ...' He stopped to sniff.

'They were tragic times for all of us,' said Mr Crutcher, opening the door to the drawing room. 'The twins are through here.'

Mr Farthing paused to judge how much he would have to stoop to avoid banging his head. 'How are they?' he asked quietly.

'They're still dreadfully affected by their parents' deaths. We all are,' said Mr Crutcher, solemnly.

'Of course.' Mr Farthing stepped into the room, banging his head on the door frame.

Lorelli and Ovid looked up from the chessboard.

'I don't want to interrupt. Please finish your game,' said Mr Farthing apologetically.

'I don't think you want to wait that long,' said Ovid, smiling. 'To date this game of chess has lasted one year, two months, fourteen days and one hour. And judging by the current status it's unlikely to conclude any time soon.'

Like everything the Thornthwaite twins did, every chess move was carefully calculated, every repercussion considered, every aspect of the game mulled over.

'It's been Lorelli's turn for several weeks,' continued Ovid.

Every so often during those weeks, Lorelli's hand would waver over a piece, her green eyes glancing at her brother. Then, seeing the tiny curl of a smile appear at the corner of his mouth, she would pull back her hand, leaving the piece untouched.

'I'll defeat him in the end,' said Lorelli. She picked up a bishop and moved it forward. 'It's merely a matter of time.'

Mr Farthing looked unsure how to respond to this and was pleased when Mr Crutcher said, 'This is Bernard Farthing, the family lawyer.'

'Please sit down, Mr Farthing,' said Ovid.

The lawyer squeezed his wide hips into a chair.

'I'll send for tea,' said Mr Crutcher, ringing a bell in the corner of the room.

Mr Farthing placed his case on the desk, clicked it open and withdrew a plastic folder from which he extracted a single piece of yellowing paper. He unfolded it gently, careful not to tear it where the paper had thinned along the folds.

'Is that it?' asked Lorelli. 'Is that the will?'

'It is.'

'Can I look at it?' asked Ovid.

'Of course you are entitled to read it,' replied the lawyer, 'but I'm afraid it's all very technical legal jargon. Essentially it says that the family inheritance be divided between the two of you on your sixteenth birthday.'

'Yes, we know that,' said Lorelli impatiently. 'We'd like to make an amendment.'

The door opened and Hazel entered with the tea. Mr Crutcher relieved her of the tea tray and she left the room. He brought the tray to the table and began to pour.

'You've employed a new maid since my last visit,' observed Mr Farthing.

'Hazel? No, she's Mrs Bagshaw's adopted daughter,' replied Mr Crutcher. 'She would have been a baby when you last visited.'

'And she works as a maid now?'

'Mrs Bagshaw likes to keep her busy,' said Mr Crutcher.

Two years older than the twins, Hazel had also grown up in the gloom of Thornthwaite Manor, rarely speaking, never making eye contact with anyone and unquestioningly doing whatever Mrs Bagshaw told her to do.

'What adjustment do you want to make to the will?' asked Mr Farthing. 'I'm afraid it's impossible to bring the date of inheritance forward.'

'We want to add a clause stating that if either of us dies before the age of sixteen, the other instantly be cut out of the will,' said Lorelli, never one to skirt around an issue.

Mr Farthing shifted uncomfortably. 'It's a most unusual clause.'

'Yes, but can you make it legally binding?' asked Lorelli.

'I suppose so, yes.'

'How long will it take?' asked Ovid.

'In order to make any addition I'll have to draw up the will from scratch, and that means I'll need to conduct a complete inventory.'

'An inventory?' said Ovid.

'Yes, you know, new legal legislation and all that. Everything has to be itemised these days.'

'How long will that take?' asked Lorelli.

Mr Farthing glanced around at the pictures, clocks and antiques which filled the hall. 'How many rooms does the manor have?'

Mr Crutcher stepped forward. 'Eighty-seven in total,' he said with a small bow.

'My goodness.'

'Thornthwaite Manor has undergone many changes over the years. Each generation has added or altered something to suit their own needs or passions,' said Mr Crutcher.

Mr Farthing scratched his head. 'You have a lot of things to itemise, then. It will take me at least a month, I'd estimate.'

'A month?' exclaimed Ovid. 'That's a long time.'

'I'm sorry, but I'll have to come up every day and Thornthwaite Manor is a good two-hour drive from my home.'

'What if you were to come and stay with us? We have plenty of spare guest rooms, don't we,

Mr Crutcher?' said Lorelli, keen to get the matter sorted as quickly as possible.

'Certainly,' said the butler, offering the lawyer a plate of plain digestives.

'Thank you.' Mr Farthing took one and turned to Lorelli. 'Well, yes, I suppose that would speed up things,' he admitted. 'As it happens, I'm having some work done on my house and it would be nice to get out for a while.'

'Then it's decided,' said Lorelli before her brother could make any further objection. 'Mr Farthing will come and stay with us while he makes his inventory.'

THE LAWYER'S SON

Thornthwaite Manor received very few visitors, so the next morning, when Lorelli and Ovid heard the sound of gravel beneath tyres, they ran to an upstairs window and watched as the lawyer's old, rusty, dust-coloured car pulled up outside.

'I don't see why he has to come and live with us,' said Ovid, who didn't like the idea of a stranger staying in Thornthwaite Manor.

'Don't you want this settled as soon as possible?' replied Lorelli.

'I suppose so, but I don't trust him.'

The car door opened and Mr Farthing stepped out.

'You don't trust anyone,' countered Lorelli with a smile.

Mr Farthing lifted four large suitcases from the boot.

'You think he's got enough luggage?' said Ovid.

'I don't think it's all his,' said Lorelli, seeing the

passenger door open and a fair-haired boy step out. He was tall like his father but unlike Mr Farthing he carried his size with confidence. He slammed the door and stood back to look up at the house, shielding his eyes from the sun.

Instinctively, both twins moved back from the window. The doorbell rang. They glanced at each other and ran to the stairs, where they could see the front door in the reflection of a convex mirror.

Mr Crutcher opened the door and said in his usual solemn tone, 'Bernard, welcome.'

'Alfred,' said Mr Farthing, 'allow me to introduce my son, Adam.'

'Pleased to meet you, sir,' said the boy, leaning forward and offering his hand.

Mr Crutcher looked at it but made no attempt to shake it. 'You may park the car around the back,' he said.

'Can I park it?' said Adam. 'Can I dad? Please.'

'You're not old enough,' replied his father.

'It's private land,' protested Adam, 'Anyway, I'm fifteen. Only a couple of years off. Please.'

'Oh, all right.' Mr Farthing smile indulgently and handed him the keys. 'Drive carefully. Only first gear.'

'Great.' Adam bounded away and Mr Crutcher picked up his suitcase.

'I spoil him,' said Mr Farthing, 'but since his mother . . .' He faltered. 'Since then it's only been him and me, and he's such a good boy, so bright, what's a doting father to do? It is all right, his coming to stay as well, isn't it?'

'We have plenty of room,' said Mr Crutcher. 'Let me help you with your luggage.'

'Thank you, then I would like to speak to the cook. Adam has certain food allergies that I must tell her about.'

After Mr Farthing and Mr Crutcher had put the bags away and Adam had parked the car, everyone assembled in the drawing room for weak tea and sandwiches filled with some indefinable, flavourless grey paste.

Lorelli was sitting opposite Adam, watching him suspiciously, while Ovid sat at the piano, playing a mournful melody with his right hand and jarring chords with his left. Mr Farthing was studying legal documents at the table. Mr Crutcher poured the tea.

Up close, Lorelli noticed that Adam had all of the facial features that were usually listed in books when describing good-looking boys.

'Where's your TV?' asked Adam.

Mr Crutcher cleared his throat. 'In Thornthwaite Manor we live without such dangerous electronic intrusions as televisions or telephones,' he said.

'No TV, wow,' said Adam. 'Do you play the piano as well, Lorelli?' he asked enthusiastically.

'I'm afraid I have no musical ability at all,' she

replied politely. 'What about you?'

'I play a little,' he said. 'I learnt at my school, Saint Swivels. Our teacher is a world-class pianist. Saint Swivels is the best school in the country.'

Mr Farthing coughed. 'Now, son, remember what I said about bragging.'

'Why don't you play something for us now?' said Lorelli.

Hearing this Ovid stopped, his fingers remaining pressed down on the keys, causing the chord to linger in the air. He turned around on the stool and scowled at Lorelli.

She smiled innocently back at him. 'Of course you are an excellent pianist, Ovid, but sometimes I tire of the same old pieces,' she said with her usual candour. 'It would be nice to hear someone else's repertoire for a change.'

'Be my guest,' said Ovid, moving to the table, where Mr Farthing glanced up from his papers and looked at him.

'You know, you are the very image of your father,' he said. 'I mean apart from the scar, of course.'

'What scar? His portrait shows no scar,' said Ovid.

'It was a minor blemish on the bridge of his nose,' said Mr Crutcher. 'It was caused by a hunting accident. He was shooting grouse when the gun backfired. It happened after the portrait was painted.'

'Play us a tune, son,' said Mr Farthing.

Adam sat down at the piano and began to play, but instead of the sombre chords that Ovid favoured, he played bright notes and a happy melody. Lorelli had never heard anything like it. It was a joyous uplifting sound.

'Enough!' cried Mr Crutcher, darting over to the piano and slamming down the lid. Adam whipped his hands away just in time.

Neither Ovid nor Lorelli had ever witnessed Mr Crutcher angry before but there was no mistaking the fire in his eyes. He composed himself, brushed down his suit and spoke quietly. 'This piano is an antique. It is not designed for music at such a tempo. To play in such an irresponsible manner could cause great harm. Adam Farthing, while you are within these walls, you will live as we do, in sobriety and respectful mourning.'

Adam looked shaken, but composed himself and said softly, 'It's only music.'

THE BUTLER

Teacher, legal guardian and loyal servant, Alfred Crutcher played a number of parts in the twins' lives.

In spite of these seemingly conflicting roles he knew his place. He never gave the twins orders. He only ever made requests. And yet there was a subtle insistence in the requests that, a few years ago, had brought out a brief but acute rebellious streak in young Ovid Thornthwaite. Many children go through a phase of not wanting to go to school. It is only natural. Usually there is a parent to drag them out of bed and take them. However, when one sunny January morning Ovid decided he would rather go fishing than attend Mr Crutcher's maths lesson, Mr Crutcher did not demand that Ovid do as he was told. Instead, the wiry servant stood motionless, unblinking, before saying, 'It's going to rain today. I wouldn't want you to catch your death.'

'Nonsense,' replied Ovid dismissively. 'There isn't a

cloud in the sky.'

Ovid knew perfectly well how closely his head servant studied the weather and how rarely he was wrong about it. Upon closer inspection Ovid would have seen three clouds in the easterly corner of the horizon. By the time he had dressed, breakfasted and was climbing into the back of the car, those three clouds were eight and they had encroached further on the beautiful winter's sky.

Ovid was not so young as to fail to pick up on his servant's disapproval but in his youthful rebellion he ignored it. *So what if I want to go fishing?* he thought.

Mr Crutcher drove him to the far side of Avernus Lake, the huge expanse of water which lay in the furthest corner of the Thornthwaites' enormous estate. Ovid got out of the car with his fishing rod and bait.

'If you don't mind, younger master, I must get back to your sister's schooling now,' said Mr Crutcher. 'When would you like me to collect you?'

Ovid knew that there was an implied criticism in his servant's carefully chosen words and he wasn't having any of it. 'Not until the sun goes down,' he replied.

'What if it rains, sir?'

'I told you, Alfred, it's not going to rain.'

'And will sir not get hungry?'

'I have a packet of biscuits,' replied Ovid, pulling them from out of his pocket.

'How nutritious.'

'Yes, they are,' snapped the young, rebellious Ovid.

'Would sir care for his umbrella?'

'No, I would not. Now leave me alone.'

'Very well, sir,' replied his servant and he climbed into the car and drove away, leaving Ovid on the far side of the huge lake.

An hour later the last scrap of blue had disappeared from the sky, behind a blanket of thick grey cloud. Another hour passed and Ovid noticed the ripple as a drop of rain landed on the still lake. Before long the water was busy with ripples. Ovid had failed to catch a single fish and the rain was coming down hard. He searched for shelter but on that side of the lake there were precious few places to get out of the rain, which grew steadily heavier and showed no signs of easing off.

Before long Ovid's clothes were as wet as if he had been swimming in them. He made his way back home on foot. He was growing hungry and took out the packet of biscuits but had only had one soggy bite when he slipped and the packet flew from his wet hands. Muddy, hungry and soaking wet, Ovid continued the long walk.

When he finally arrived home, Mr Crutcher opened the door.

'Why didn't you come and get me?' demanded the petulant young man.

'I'm so sorry, sir,' replied the butler. 'Your sister and I became so engrossed in a mathematical problem that we did not notice the rain. Would you like me to run you a bath?'

And so ended Ovid's rebellious streak.

From then on he did not contradict Mr Crutcher.

THE ALLIANCE

Like most things in Thornthwaite Manor the twins' chess set was an antique, a family heirloom passed down from their ancestors. Instead of wooden pieces painted black and white, Lorelli and Ovid played with ones made of silver and copper on a heavy metallic board.

Ovid reached forward and moved his knight, bringing it within striking distance of Lorelli's bishop.

Lorelli frowned. 'Why are you so interested in that bishop?'

'Because it's there,' replied Ovid simply. He sat back, knowing that it would be some time before his sister responded to this move. 'I don't trust Adam Farthing,' he said.

'What, because he goes to a good school and plays the piano well?'

'You just like him because he's handsome,' said Ovid, watching his sister for a reaction.

'You think he's handsome, do you?' countered Lorelli, with a goading smile.

'I don't trust him,' said Ovid again. 'Why didn't Mr Farthing mention him when you invited him to stay? Why just turn up with him like that?'

'What do you think he's going to do? Murder us in our beds?'

'There are worse things in the world than murder.'

Lorelli smiled. 'Did it ever occur to you that perhaps Adam is exactly as he seems?'

'No one is exactly as they seem.'

'Talking of which, I saw that two boxes of rat poison were delivered today. You're not up to anything, are you?'

Ovid laughed. 'My dear sister, we have a truce. Besides, you really think I would stoop to something as crude as rat poison?'

'Then what's it for?' demanded Lorelli.

'If you don't mind, Miss Lorelli, I know.'

The voice startled both of them. Hazel was standing in the doorway, holding a tea tray.

'Hazel,' said Lorelli. 'How long have you been there?'

'I brought tea, miss,' she replied, with a careful curtsy. 'The rat poison is for the rats. Mrs Bagshaw saw one the other day and so she ordered poison. She says we can't be having no rats in the kitchen.'

'Thank you Hazel,' said Ovid as she placed the tray

on the table and poured milk into the cups.

'Yes, thank you,' said Lorelli. 'But you know, you really don't have to bring tea. You don't work for us.'

'Mrs Bagshaw says she doesn't want me succumbing to idleness, Miss Lorelli.'

'Why don't you join us?' said Lorelli, knowing what the answer would be.

'Thank you, but Mrs Bagshaw wouldn't like that.'

'She's very strict with you,' said Lorelli.

'Mrs Bagshaw has looked after me since I was a baby. She don't like you to see it, but she's always been kind to me,' said Hazel, pouring the tea.

Ovid took his cup. 'What's your opinion of Adam Farthing, Hazel?'

'I don't have an opinion as such, sir.'

'But do you think he's trustworthy?'

'Mrs Bagshaw says that he seems like a good boy. He's already offered to help her with the food preparations. She said no, of course. She don't let anyone help in that way, but she said she liked being asked.'

'Yes, but what do you think?'

Hazel considered for a moment. 'I agree that he's very handsome and he is helpful. I was making the tea just now and, without even being asked, he warmed the teapot for me.'

'Handsome, helpful, musical, charming . . . Sounds too good to be true, don't you think?' asked Ovid.

'I'm sure I don't know, Master Ovid,' replied Hazel.

'May I go now?'

'Of course,' replied Ovid dismissively.

Hazel left the room.

'You should be kinder to her,' said Lorelli, sipping her tea. 'She and the other servants are the only family we have.'

'Apart from each other,' Ovid replied. 'And that's what I wanted to say to you. Now that we have a more friendly arrangement I think we should remain united when it comes to outsiders.'

'You mean outsiders like Adam Farthing?'

'Yes, exactly like Adam Farthing,' responded Ovid.

'So what do you suggest?'

'An alliance.'

'And what would this alliance involve?'

'It would involve the two of us staying strong and ensuring that no one comes along and ruins our truce.'

Lorelli laughed. 'Truces, alliances, I don't know what's come over you recently.'

'But you'll agree to it?' asked Ovid.

'I have no interest in befriending Adam Farthing but I will be civil to him. Now if you don't mind, I'm going for a swim,' Lorelli stated.

AVERNUS LAKE

As a young girl, Lorelli Thornthwaite was haunted by a recurring nightmare in which she was drowning in Avernus Lake. In the dream, whenever her head was above water, she thrashed her limbs wildly in panic and desperation, but as her head went under she was overcome with a strange feeling of calm and peacefulness, as her lungs filled with water and she felt her life ebbing away.

Whereas this dream would have given most people a terrible fear of water, Lorelli, with characteristic practicality, requested swimming lessons. Mr Crutcher decided that old Tom Paine, the gardener, was best qualified to teach her, being a strong swimmer himself.

For weeks, Tom took Lorelli down to the shallowest corner of the lake and taught her how to swim, until one day, she said, 'I think I'm ready now.'

'Ready for what, miss?' asked Tom.

'To swim across the lake,' replied the young Lorelli.

'Excuse me miss?'

'I want to swim across Avernus Lake.'

'I see,' replied Tom.

Old Tom Paine believed that children should be treated like plants. Although feeding and tending was necessary, it was Tom's opinion that being left to their own devices was what they required to grow properly.

As a safety precaution he persuaded Lorelli to allow him to row alongside in case she got tired.

As it happened, this was unnecessary. Lorelli barely even shivered as she stepped into the icy waters. Keeping her head high above the surface, she crossed the lake with the greatest of ease.

Since then she had swum across the lake and back every day, except during the winter months when the water was too cold even for her.

This year had been a long cold winter that had stretched its icy fingers as far as April. Not until this, the first day of the Easter holidays, was it warm enough to swim. It was a day Lorelli always looked forward to, but it was still bitterly cold, so she put on a warm coat before heading down to the lake.

At the lakeside, she took off her coat and stripped down to her swimming costume, shivering as a cold wind blew against her exposed skin. She quickly dipped her legs then the rest of her body into the lake and instantly felt better. The coldness of the water was different somehow to that of the air. She liked it. Once fully immersed, Lorelli swam confidently across the lake.

On her way back, she felt extremely relaxed. Listening to the lapping water in her ears and the sound of her own breathing, all thoughts and worries disappeared from her head.

Then, as she reached the centre of the lake, she felt an icy chill spread through her body. But it wasn't the comforting numbness from the cold water. This was different. Her arms and legs seized up entirely. As her head sank under the surface, she tried to cry out but water filled her mouth.

Her arms and legs were useless. She tried to fill her lungs with air, remembering that this way her body was more likely to float but, without the use of her limbs, she sank helplessly into the deep water, resurfacing long enough to scream for help before slipping under once more.

Sinking down into the depths of the lake, Lorelli didn't see the tall fair-haired boy on the lakeside tear off his coat and dive in.

THE RESCUE

Although Lorelli Thornthwaite prided herself on having a good knowledge of the sorts of books that were widely regarded as classics of English literature, she had also spent enough time reading trashy romances to be familiar with the etiquette of having been rescued from a near-death experience by a handsome young man.

The heroines in those books would have gazed into Adam Farthing's blue eyes, thrown their arms around his neck and kissed him.

Lorelli did none these things. She sat upright on the lake shore and, once she had got her breath back, said, 'That was very kind of you, Adam. Thank you.'

'You're welcome,' replied Adam, matching her polite tone. 'Why were you swimming on such a cold day?'

'I swim whenever I can,' stated Lorelli, rubbing her legs and feeling them come back to life.

Adam helped her to her feet. Lorelli felt very aware of his arm around her waist. She wriggled free of his grip, and found the towel and clothes she had left by the shore of the lake. She dried herself and quickly dressed to get warm, handing the towel to Adam. He dried his hair but there was nothing he could do about his soaking clothes.

'What happened?' asked Adam.

Lorelli explained the strange sensation of losing feeling in her arms and legs. 'I can't understand it,' she said. 'I've never had that problem before.'

'Sounds like you experienced EHMS. It stands for Extreme Hypothermic Muscle Seizure.'

'I've never heard of it.'

'It's quite common. I read about it in a medical book,' said Adam. 'I read lots of medical books. When I grow up, I'm going to be a doctor.'

As they walked back to the house, a bitter wind blew and Lorelli felt sorry for Adam shivering in his damp clothes.

'Fell in the lake, did you?' said Tom Paine, who was strolling purposefully in the opposite direction, carrying his beekeeper's hat under one arm.

'Actually I jumped in,' replied Adam.

'Bit cold for swimmin'.'

'He was saving me from drowning,' said Lorelli.

'Oh aye.'

'I was taking a walk around the lake when I heard

her scream,' said Adam.

'Lucky you were there, then,' said Tom.

'Yes, it was,' said Adam. 'Actually, I'm glad we've run into you. I was wondering whether it would be possible to take one of the horses out riding? I saw you had stables.'

'They aren't my horses, Master Farthing. You'd have to ask one of the twins for permission.'

Adam turned to Lorelli. 'Perhaps you could come with me. We could make a day of it and go to Little Fledgling.'

Lorelli considered this. She remembered Ovid's desire for an alliance against Adam, but that was before he had saved her. The thought of a trip to the village chilled her blood even more than the cold water of Avernus Lake, so she was surprised to hear herself reply, 'All right, then.'

LITTLE FLEDGLING

The village of Little Fledgling in the county of Hexford stood two miles south of Thornthwaite Manor, although, as local historians liked to explain, it used to be much nearer.

In the late eighteenth century, the land was owned by Lord Milton Thornthwaite, whose portrait showed a man with deep-set eyes and skeletal cheekbones. At that time the village was situated on the far side of the apple orchard, where Avernus Lake now lay. Lord Milton detested having peasants living so near, believing them to be unclean and insolent. He charged the villagers such high land tax that the village was one of the poorest in the country. As a consequence, local boys frequently stole apples from the orchard, which only proved to Lord Milton that his low opinion of the poor was well founded.

The thefts continued even after the introduction of public floggings, so in an act of final exasperation,

Lord Milton had each house in the village knocked down and the village moved to a more suitable site on the other side of the River Curtail. A deep hole was dug and Avernus Lake was made where the village had originally stood, ensuring that no future settlements could spring up so close to the orchard and the manor.

After this, the relationship between landowner and villagers declined still further and remained poor with subsequent generations of Thornthwaites.

Lorelli and Ovid had only ever visited the village once, several years ago. They had badgered Mr Crutcher for months to take them there. They had been very young at the time and were desperate to expand their knowledge of the world. Mr Crutcher eventually succumbed and agreed to take them on 5th November to watch the village bonfire-night celebrations.

He couldn't have picked a worse time. It may have been because Mr Crutcher himself rarely went into Little Fledgling that he was unaware of the local custom, peculiar to that village.

It is common in most parts of England to burn Guy Fawkes on 5th November in remembrance of his failed attempt to blow up the Houses of Parliament, but in some parts of the country other figures are burnt. In Lewes in Sussex, effigies of the pope, as well as topical personalities, are burnt. In Little Fledgling, it had always been the tradition to burn a doll made to look like a Thornthwaite.

And so it was that on the twins' one and only visit to their local village they stood in a crowd of people as a life-sized figure with black-wool hair and green-button eyes was thrown on to a fire, while all around rejoiced.

For the two young, black-haired, green-eyed twins it seemed as though they had been transported back to the Middle Ages and were watching an angry mob of witch-burners.

For the first and last time in their lives the twins clung on to each other for protection, convinced that if they were noticed the crowd would turn on them. 'Shall I take you home now?' Mr Crutcher said before leading them through the crowd and driving them back down the road, over Beryl's Bridge and to the safety and sanctuary provided by Thornthwaite Manor. Both twins cried all the way home.

The next day, Lorelli narrowly avoided being killed by a stray arrow, while Ovid was practising his archery skills, and Ovid nearly met his end when some exceptionally poisonous berries found their way into his porridge.

Life was back to normal.

THE INVENTORY

Many twins claim to have a telepathic connection. They say that while one is experiencing an emotion such as joy or misery, even if they are separated, the other feels it too.

Ovid and Lorelli had never felt any such connection. Usually the opposite was true. While one was experiencing pain or discomfort, the other was generally having an extremely good time, often having been the cause of their sibling's distress. Like the time that Lorelli accidentally consumed a rare tropical poison, while Ovid was in the hothouse, happily tending his collection of rare tropical plants.

However, unbeknown to either twin, at the exact same time that Lorelli lost the ability to swim, Ovid felt dizzy and had to sit down in the corner of the portrait room, while the sensation passed.

Ovid was sitting so quietly that Mr Farthing failed to notice him as he entered. The large lawyer walked across the room. He stopped in front of the portrait of Ovid's parents and stared at it.

'Is that part of the inventory?' said Ovid, feeling energy return to his limbs.

'What? Who's that?' Mr Farthing sounded startled. He turned and Ovid could see that his face was wet. He pulled out a handkerchief and wiped away his tears. 'Ovid, my dear boy, you almost scared me to death.'

'Why are you crying?'

'Lord and Lady Thornthwaite died around the same time as my dear wife and it brings it all back. Grief is a terrible thing.'

'I see. Shouldn't you be busy with your inventory?' Ovid was uncomfortable with Mr Farthing's sudden display of emotion.

'Yes, well, this is all part of the process. Everything must be accounted for,' replied Mr Farthing, sounding flustered. He opened his briefcase, accidentally spilling its contents on the floor. Kneeling down to pick up the bits of paper, he asked nervously, 'Were you spying on me?'

'Should I be?' replied Ovid.

For a moment the lawyer seemed taken aback with Ovid's question. 'Well, no. I must get on with my job,' he said, the anger in his tone taking Ovid by surprise. The lawyer smiled apologetically. 'I am sorry to have snapped. I realise you are merely curious, but I must assure you that it is all very routine. They bring in these new rules all the time that make more work for us and I don't know who benefits. Take my advice, when you grow up, don't become a lawyer.'

'I have no intention of doing so,' said Ovid, leaving Mr Farthing alone in the portrait room.

THE NURSE

Nurse Griddle had a large nose with such cavernous nostrils that Lorelli and Ovid often wondered whether she was actually capable of smelling illness. She certainly had a knack of turning up whenever there was something amiss with one of them.

A tall woman with short hair and broad shoulders, she was remarkable in that as long as the twins had known her, she had never once smiled. Never out of politeness, nor out of sympathy. Not with compassion, nor with amusement. Smiling was not something she did.

As the sodden Lorelli and Adam approached the mansion, Nurse Griddle flung open the door, took one look at them and said, 'You will both come with me now.'

Lorelli whispered to Adam, 'It's best to do as she says.'

They followed Nurse Griddle inside and down the

stairs to the windowless room in which rows of shelves were lined with medicines, lotions, bandages, plasters, pills and medical books.

Nurse Griddle picked up two sterile thermometers and thrust them into Lorelli and Adam's mouths. Adam tried to take his out but Nurse Griddle stopped him. She grabbed a towel from a drawer and gave it to him to keep warm.

'You have both been swimming in that lake,' she said. 'I have come to expect such madness from Lorelli, but I am surprised at you, Adam Farthing. Mrs Bagshaw said you were a sensible young man.'

With thermometers in their mouths, neither Adam nor Lorelli were able to respond.

'That lake is far more dangerous than it looks,' continued Nurse Griddle. 'It has taken its fair share of lives over the years and it wouldn't think twice about taking yours.'

She whipped out the thermometers. 'Well,' she said, examining them, 'you both seem all right. What have you to say for yourselves?'

'It wasn't Adam's fault,' said Lorelli. 'I was swimming across when my arms and legs froze stiff. I don't know why . . .'

'Froze stiff?'

'Adam said it sounded like EHMS,' said Lorelli.

'Extreme Hypothermic Muscle Seizure,' said Adam.

'Never heard of such a thing,' said Nurse Griddle.

'I read it in a medical book. I'm going to be a doctor when I grow up,' said Adam.

'If you want to be anything at all when you grow up, I suggest you stay away from that lake, both of you.'

Lorelli had no intention of staying away from her favourite pastime but she was interested in something else that Nurse Griddle had said. 'What lives has the lake claimed?' she asked. 'I've never heard of anyone dying in it.'

Nurse Griddle shut the door.

'I am only telling you this because I hope it will make you realise how dangerous the lake is,' she said quietly. 'Years ago, there were two young men drinking in the village pub when one evening, after several strong beers, one of them bet the other that he could swim across Avernus Lake quicker than the other could run around it. Being drunk and foolish, the other accepted the bet and they set off down to the lake, along with half the pub, who gathered around to watch. It was dark but lots of them carried torches. The foolish man stripped down to his underwear and his friend took off his jacket. The landlord of the pub blew a whistle and the race began. There was much shouting as the onlookers followed the second man around the lake. When he reached the other side before his friend, there was a great cheer. They waited for the other man to arrive at the far shore. They shone their torches over the lake but could see no one. Someone found a boat and a few of them, including the man's friend, headed out to find him, but they never did. The sun came up. The police were called, the lake was searched, but they never found any trace of the man.'

'Then he might have survived,' said Lorelli. 'I mean, if no one found him.'

Nurse Griddle shook her head. 'That lake is deeper than you think. I have never liked the idea of you swimming across it and now that this has happened perhaps you will learn your lesson. Now, both of you go and take hot baths and I will bring you my warming remedy.'

THE LIBRARY

Lorelli wasn't sure if it was a symptom of what had happened in the lake or the effect of Nurse Griddle's story but, even after the hot bath and a cup of the warming remedy she couldn't shake the chilled feeling in her bones, so she went to the library.

It was, without a doubt, her favourite room in the whole of Thornthwaite Manor. Its high walls were lined with books dating back centuries, although none purchased since her parents had died. Nurse Griddle had asked Mr Crutcher to buy new titles for Lorelli to read but it was his opinion that until she had read the existing books, new ones would only be a waste of money.

Whenever Lorelli felt sad or lonely, she would go to the library and walk around the walls, with one hand outstretched so that she felt the ridges of the book spines, as though she could touch all the different worlds that these books represented through her fingertips.

As usual she found herself stopping at the familiar spine of her favourite novel, The Seven Dances of Franciska Tóth by Imelda Gaunt. She had never spoken to anyone about it, certainly not Ovid, who would have stolen it had he known how much she loved the story. She had toyed with asking Nurse Griddle to look in the village library for any other books by the author, but she never did. Keeping it to herself made the book and its story all the more precious. Each novel she read was like a sanctuary where she could hide, and Imelda Gaunt's was a world away from the one in which she lived. It was a place which belonged entirely to her.

Hearing the library door open, Lorelli replaced the book and took another from the shelf.

'I'll never understand what you get out of all this make-believe,' said Ovid.

'I get to escape,' replied Lorelli.

'I hear you only narrowly escaped death this morning.'

'Yes, if Adam hadn't been there your troubles would be over and you would be the sole heir to the inheritance.'

'My dear sister, we have a truce and, I should remind you, an alliance.'

'I'm fed up of your stupid games,' Lorelli snapped.

'You trust Adam Farthing now he's saved your life, do you?'

'It seems like a perfectly good reason to trust someone.'

'Unless they slipped something in your drink precisely so they could save you.'

'You're being ridiculous.' Lorelli put the book she was holding back on the shelf.

'Am I?' asked Ovid. 'I felt dizzy this morning too. And you heard what Hazel said about Mr Helpful warming the pot for her.'

'This is ridiculous. I don't believe you. You're just trying to turn me against Adam. The world isn't full of mysteries and murderers. Some people are just as they appear and Adam Farthing is one of them. He's friendly and kind and normal. I want to be like that too. We've spent all our lives trying to kill each other. You think that's normal? It's not.'

'You're being a fool.'

'No!' yelled Lorelli. 'You're jealous of Adam and you don't want me to be friends with him because you're worried that I'll realise how much nicer he is than you. Well, it's too late. I've already realised.'

'Ah-hem.'

The twins turned to find Mr Crutcher standing in the doorway.

'Young master and young mistress, I am terribly sorry to interrupt but I heard raised voices and, as you both know, raised voices are not allowed in the library.' He pointed to a sign on the wall that said, *Quiet Please!*

'I also came to say that dinner will be ready in ten minutes. Both Mr Farthing and his son will be joining you for your evening meal.'

'Thank you, Alfred,' said Ovid.

'Yes, thank you. We're coming now,' said Lorelli.

THE COOK

In stark contrast to the other servants at Thornthwaite Manor, Mrs Bagshaw, the cook was one of the most naturally and relentlessly cheerful people in the world. She always had a smile for the twins, and reserved all her strict words for Hazel. A number of years ago, the twins had become interested in how she had come to adopt Hazel, but Mrs Bagshaw had not been forthcoming with an answer. In the end, it was Tom Paine, the gardener, who had told them the story.

'Mrs Bagshaw didn't always live at Thornthwaite Manor,' Tom had told them. 'She used to rent a cottage in the village from your father. Bagshaw's End, she called it. This was before you were born, before Nurse Griddle joined us even. Mrs B. lived there with her husband, Hedley Bagshaw. He worked at the printing press in the village, where they print the *Hexford Express*. In his spare time he was a local historian. The paper published his articles sometimes.

'Mrs Bagshaw only took a job here to earn a little extra money until she began a family of her own, but things don't always go the way you expect them, particularly not when planning families. Years passed and there was still no child. Eventually, I guess they gave up. Then one night, with Hedley working late at the printing press, Mrs Bagshaw was alone in the house when there was a knock at the door. She answered it and found a beautiful baby girl with a note asking her to look after her.'

'Who left it?' Lorelli asked.

'She never knew. So she picked up the child and rushed down to the printer's to tell Hedley what had happened.'

'Wasn't he there?' asked Ovid, trying to guess the story.

'He was there all right,' said Tom, 'only he was dead. Hedley Bagshaw had tripped and fallen into the printing press. When they finally recovered him, the man who spent his life printing the news was dead with the next day's news printed all over his body. Mrs Bagshaw never recovered from that.'

The twins felt sad for Mrs Bagshaw but also found it comforting that the one cheery person in their vicinity harboured a past as dark and upsetting as their own.

'Adam tells me you had something of an adventure today, Lorelli,' said Mr Farthing as the twins took their places at the table.

'If you call almost dying an adventure, then yes,' replied Lorelli.

'Thank goodness Adam was there to save you.' Mr Farthing looked proudly at his son.

'It was incredible good fortune, wasn't it,' said Ovid.

Mr Crutcher entered holding a large bowl of soup, closely followed by Hazel with a basket of bread.

'To start, two-potato soup,' announced Mr Crutcher, using a ladle to fill everyone's bowls.

'What's in it?' asked Mr Farthing.

'Two potatoes,' said Mr Crutcher flatly. 'And I daresay, knowing Mrs Bagshaw, a pinch of salt,' he added.

'Good. I have informed your cook that Adam has a number of severe food allergies, but one can't be too careful, you know,' explained Mr Farthing.

'You shouldn't fuss so,' said Adam.

Mr Farthing took one of the bread rolls Hazel was handing round and accidentally dropped it into his soup.

'You're such a clumsy oaf, Dad.' Adam grinned. He took a roll, tore a piece off, and popped it in his mouth.

'Now now, son,' said Mr Farthing, embarrassed.

Suddenly the smile fell from Adam's face and the bread roll fell from his fist. He shot a hand up to his throat and gasped, 'Can't breathe ... my throat ... my ...'

Mr Farthing jumped up, knocking his bowl over,

spilling the contents over the table. 'What is it? What is it, son?' he asked.

'I'll fetch Nurse Griddle,' said Mr Crutcher.

'What else was in those rolls?' demanded Mr Farthing angrily, snatching the basket from Hazel.

'Just a few nuts, sir.'

'Nuts?' Mr Farthing placed his son on the cold wooden floor. 'He has a fatal allergy to nuts, you idiot girl. You've killed my son.'

Hazel screamed and fell to the floor in tears.

'Fetch the nurse,' cried Mr Farthing.

'I'm already here. Stand back,' said Nurse Griddle, dashing into the room.

AT LEAST ONE WEAKNESS

'Do you have his EpiPen?' said Nurse Griddle.

'His what?' said Mr Farthing.

'His EpiPen. Surely you carry one if your son has such bad allergies.'

'Oh, his syringe thingy, yes.' Mr Farthing opened his briefcase but was too flustered to find anything so Nurse Griddle snatched it off him and pulled out the EpiPen, took off the wrapper, held it to Adam's leg and pushed down on the top.

Adam gasped.

'What are you doing?' asked Lorelli.

'This will revive him,' Nurse Griddle explained. 'It should reverse the symptoms of the reaction. Mr Crutcher, fetch the stretcher.'

The stretcher was brought and Adam was carried away by Mr Crutcher and Mr Farthing, with Nurse Griddle close behind.

Ovid took his place back at the table.

'How can you think about food now?' said Lorelli.

'There's no point letting the soup go cold,' he replied.

Hazel had stood up and retreated to the corner of the room, avoiding eye contact with the twins.

'It wasn't your fault, Hazel,' said Lorelli, 'you weren't to know he was allergic to nuts.'

'Yes, miss,' replied Hazel, keeping her eyes focused on the floor.

Mrs Bagshaw entered the room. 'What's happening?' she said. 'I heard a commotion. Where is everyone?'

'Adam had an allergic reaction to the nuts in the bread mix, but Nurse Griddle stopped him from dying,' said Ovid succinctly.

Mrs Bagshaw turned to look at Hazel. 'You put nuts in the bread mix? How could you have done such a thing? Mr Farthing told me on his first day about his son's allergy.'

'I didn't know,' said Hazel. 'You didn't tell me.'

'I didn't know you would go and do a stupid thing like this. What on earth possessed you?'

'Nuts make it taste nicer,' said Hazel.

'I agree,' said Ovid, breaking a piece of bread, dipping it in the soup and taking a bite.

If the tiniest whisper of a smile crossed Hazel's face, it didn't last long enough for it to be noticed by Mrs Bagshaw, who said, 'You are in such trouble, Hazel

Bagshaw. Now go downstairs and prepare the main course.'

Hazel left the room and Mrs Bagshaw said, 'Now, I'll go and apologise to Mr Farthing. You two may finish off your starter. Hazel will bring up the next course shortly.'

Lorelli sat down opposite Ovid.

'Just the two of us again,' her brother said.

'I don't see why you find this so amusing,' said Lorelli. 'Adam could have died.'

Ovid's smile widened as he reached over the table and grabbed the half a roll that Adam had left. 'I'm smiling because Adam Farthing has shown us something tonight,' he said. 'He's shown us that he has at least one weakness.'

PRIDE AND JOY

Lorelli and Ovid had expected Adam's episode with the nuts to put him out of action for a couple of days, so they were surprised when he came bounding in for breakfast the next morning looking bright-eyed and brimming with enthusiasm and energy. He was wearing a pair of spotless white jodhpurs and carrying a black riding hat.

'Morning Lorelli,' he said, beaming.

'Are you feeling better?' Lorelli asked.

'Two hundred per cent. Thank heavens for Nurse Griddle and my EpiPen. I might have died.'

'Thank heavens,' said Ovid drily.

'And what a beautiful morning it is. It's a fine day for a ride to the village,' continued Adam, oblivious to Ovid's sarcasm.

'A ride to the village?' said Ovid, buttering a slice of toast.

'Yes, Lorelli said she would come with me.' He

turned to her. 'You're still up for it, aren't you?'

'Of course,' she said, avoiding her brother's gaze.

'I went for a run this morning and asked Tom to saddle the horses. Which will you ride?'

'You should ride Pride,' said Lorelli. 'I don't think you could handle Joy.'

The names that Tom Paine had given the horses indicated how much he loved the animals. Pride was a chocolate-brown gelding. Joy was a piebald mare.

'Why's that?' asked Adam.

'Pride is slow but dependable. Joy can get a little over-excited,' said Lorelli.

'I don't mind riding Joy,' said Adam. 'At Saint Swivels we ride every week, so I know what I'm doing.'

'Yes, let him ride Joy. He knows what he's doing,' said Ovid, taking a bite of toast.

'Like you did?' said Lorelli.

'I think I'll take my breakfast into the conservatory,' said Ovid, standing up and leaving.

'Is he all right?' said Adam.

'Ovid fell off Joy when he was little and hasn't been on a horse since,' Lorelli explained.

'Well, that's a mistake. You should always get back on immediately after a fall otherwise the fear sets in.'

After changing into her riding gear, Lorelli met Adam at the front of the manor and they walked down to the stables. Adam was right. It was a glorious day. Tom already had both horses saddled up and ready to go when she and Adam got there.

'Mornin', miss,' said Tom.

'Morning Tom,' replied Lorelli.

'So, is this one mine?' said Adam, patting Joy.

'Ridden before, have you?' said Tom.

'Oh yes, I was telling Lorelli. We have riding lessons at Saint Swivels every Friday.'

Tom looked doubtfully at Adam. 'Joy can be a bit of a handful.'

'Don't worry about me.' Adam placed a foot in the stirrup and swung himself up. Landing in the saddle, he was suddenly caught by a sneezing fit, which caused Joy to whinny in protest. Once he had got control over his sneezes and the horse he said, 'I'm sorry, it must be hay fever.'

'Isn't it a bit early in the year for hay fever?' said Lorelli.

'It seems to get earlier every year,' said Adam, pulling out a tissue and blowing his nose.

'Just to warn you, Joy's a bit nappy,' said Tom.

Adam looked confused. 'What? Like sleepy?'

'It means that she likes to go home,' said Lorelli.

'Oh yes,' said Adam.

'And she likes to eat the flowers,' said Tom.

Lorelli mounted Pride and they set off.

'Don't forget to adjust the girth before you get too far,' called Tom.

As they rode out side by side, Lorelli was nervous about the thought of making polite conversation but Adam turned out to be extremely pleasant company. In spite of herself she began to relax. She even laughed when Adam tried to slow his horse down by talking to her rather than tugging on her reins.

'What did they teach you at St Swivels?' she joked.

Adam smiled. 'The horses at St Swivels are trained to respond to your voice.'

They stopped at the top of a hilly field leading up from Avernus Lake and looked back at the view of Thornthwaite Manor nestling at the base of a wooded hill.

'Those are Huxley Woods,' said Lorelli, tugging on Pride's rein to hold her still. 'And that's Orwell Hill.' She pointed to a rocky cliff at the top where the ground suddenly fell away. 'That cliff's called Devil's Leap.'

'Devil's Leap?' said Adam. 'That's Devil's Leap?'

'Yes. Have you heard of it?'

Adam's usual sunny demeanour vanished and there was no trace of a smile when he replied, 'That's where my mother was killed.'

'Killed?'

'The police said it was suicide but I know she wouldn't leave me on purpose.'

'Who would want to kill her?'

'I don't know his name but I know his face. When she died, I saved all the drawings she did. She was a great artist, my mum. There were pictures of me and dad and self-portraits too, but mostly there was the face of the stranger. She must have drawn him twenty times or more. I believe that if I find this man I'll find my mother's murderer.'

'But didn't the police try to find out who was in the picture?'

'They never thought it was anything but suicide but one day I'll find out who killed my mother,' said Adam angrily. He rode ahead, so that she couldn't see his face, but Lorelli could tell from the way he drew a tissue from his pocket and blew his nose, that he was crying.

'We should check the girths in case they've come loose,' she said, climbing down from her horse.

Adam was by the hedge at the top of the field, pulling on Joy's rein, trying to stop her eating the brightly coloured crocuses in the meadow.

'What is that?' He looked up and pointed.

Lorelli led Pride up to the top of the field and looked over the hedge. It looked like a dark cloud hovering across the meadow. For a moment they both stood staring at it, then they heard a low humming that grew louder as the thick cloud got nearer.

'It sounds like . . . buzzing,' said Adam.

'Bees!' exclaimed Lorelli. 'And they're coming this way.'

THE SWARM OF BEES

The buzzing of the bees swarming towards Lorelli and Adam sounded like an aeroplane flying low overhead.

'Get down,' said Lorelli, ducking behind the hedge.

Before Adam could do the same, Joy looked up from the flowers she was munching and saw the bees. Panic struck, she kicked her legs in the air and whinnied.

'Adam!' shouted Lorelli.

Adam clung tightly on to the horse as she turned and ran at full pelt down the hill.

Lorelli stayed behind the hedge as the massive swarm of bees flew over her head in pursuit of Adam and Joy.

Joy was charging as fast as she could and Adam looked like he was fighting hard to avoid being thrown over her head.

Lorelli climbed on to Pride's back and headed after him. She could see that Joy's girth had wobbled itself loose and the saddle was rocking dangerously from side to side as the horse pelted down the field. The swarm of bees was gaining on them.

Lorelli watched as Joy took control of the situation. The horse came to a sudden stop and bucked her back legs up. The girth broke and the saddle fell to the ground, sending Adam flying into the lake with a splash. Finally free of her burden, Joy galloped away.

The swarm of bees meanwhile seemed interested in neither the horse nor the rider. Instead they swooped down towards the saddle.

Keeping her distance, Lorelli jumped off Pride and reached out a hand to Adam.

'No thanks,' he said, treading water, 'I feel safer here. I've never seen bees do that before.'

Lorelli looked at the saddle. It was covered in bees, crawling all over each other.

'I'm going to swim around the side and get out over by that tree in case they go for me again,' said Adam. 'You should get away too.'

'I'll meet you there,' replied Lorelli, watching Adam swim away. But instead of mounting Pride she reached into his saddle bag and pulled out a rusty old tin in which Tom stored sugar to feed to the horses as treats. She prised it open. There was one sugar cube inside, which she gave to Pride. She edged nearer to the bees, feeling nervous. Adam was right. Bees didn't usually act like this.

She bent down and held the tin wide open. It didn't take long for one of the bees to become interested in the sugary tin. Thankfully the rest remained occupied with the underside of the saddle. Lorelli waited until the bee landed inside before slamming it shut. As she moved away, she noticed that the bees who were now leaving the saddle had thick globules of yellow substance over their legs.

She climbed on to Pride's back and rode round to where a very wet Adam was crawling up the muddy shore. 'I don't understand it,' he said. 'Why did those bees go for that saddle?'

'Because the underside was covered in pollen,' replied Lorelli. 'That's why you sneezed when you first got on.'

Adam took a moment to consider this.

'But it was Tom who saddled the horses.' He clicked his fingers and added, 'And he keeps bees.'

'I've known Tom all my life. He wouldn't hurt a fly,' said Lorelli.

'Well, he knew I was riding Joy and he knew which direction we were heading.'

'He'd never do anything to hurt one of the horses.'

'Well, it seems to me that he's trying to do more than that. For some reason Tom Paine is out to get me,' said Adam.

THE GARDENER

Alfred Crutcher may have been the late Lord Thornthwaite's most trusted servant, but Tom Paine, the gardener, was the longest serving. Old Tom was the only employee at Thornthwaite Manor old enough to have worked for three generations of the family.

When his parents died and his family home was destroyed in a gas explosion, the young Tom Paine was left alone in the world. He would have been taken into care by the local authorities had Lord Silas Thornthwaite, the twins' grandfather, not taken him under his wing. This act of benevolence was so uncharacteristic that there had been a great deal of speculation among the staff at the time that there was some connection between them. Some suggested that Tom knew a secret about Silas. Others claimed that Tom was Silas's son. But as time passed, so did the rumours and Tom settled into his job as gardener, living in a small cottage in the grounds.

Tom served Silas until his death, then continued to work under the twins' father, Mycroft Thornthwaite, until he and his wife also died.

Being an orphan himself, he was the best equipped to understand how the deaths of the late Lord and Lady Thornthwaite had affected the twins and yet he never once spoke to them about their grief.

As well as managing the vast grounds and looking after the horses, he somehow still found time to keep bees. The highlight of his year was putting his honey into the local village fête. No one could remember a year when his honey hadn't won first prize.

Tom was very protective of the horses, so he felt a huge sense of relief when, not long after Adam had ridden out on Joy she came galloping back to the stables, albeit without her saddle or her rider.

Tom fed Joy a sugar cube and climbed on to her, bareback. He rode her until he found Adam and Lorelli walking across a field, leading Pride behind them.

'Jumped in the water again, did you?' said Tom, looking at Adam's wet clothes.

'No, I fell,' replied Adam. 'What were you playing at putting pollen under the saddle? Is that your idea of some sort of joke?'

'Pollen?' said Tom. 'You'll have to excuse me but I don't know anything about any pollen.'

Lorelli explained what had happened, to which

Tom said, 'No wonder Joy looked so frightened, poor love.' He patted the horse's side affectionately.

'Never mind her,' said Adam. 'I could have died.'

'If you think I'd do anything to hurt my Joy, you'd better think again, Master Farthing,' replied Tom.

'But they're your bees, aren't they?'

'That I can't tell you. Not until I've seen one.'

Lorelli handed Tom the tin. 'There's one in there.'

Tom took it and pulled it open. Adam stood back. Inside, the bee was still crawling around the sugar. Before it noticed that it had an opportunity to escape Tom slammed the tin shut again.

'Well, I never,' he said.

'What?' said Lorelli.

'That's not one of mine. If I'm not mistaken that's an Africanised bee.'

'A what?' said Adam.

'Africanised bees are hybrids of African honey bees and European honey bees,' Tom explained. 'They were originally bred in South America but I've never heard of any on this side of the Atlantic. They're more aggressive than our honey bees and they tend to swarm. Some people call them killer bees.'

'Killer bees?' said Adam.

'Apparently they've been known to sting people to death. Of course, like all bees, they'll still only sting you if they feel threatened.'

'What are they doing here?' said Adam.

'I'm afraid you've got me there,' said Tom.

Lorelli could tell by the look on Adam's face that he didn't believe Tom, but she could no more suspect Tom than she could suspect herself. The whole thing led to one conclusion. Ovid was back to his usual tricks.

THE HOTHOUSE

Back at the manor Adam went to ask Nurse Griddle for a cup of her warming remedy before changing into dry clothes. Lorelli headed up the spiral staircase to her bedroom to change out of her jodhpurs, then went to find her brother. She found him in the hothouse, tending to his tropical plants.

Although it was cold outside, the sunlight through the glass walls made the overgrown room hot and sticky. Lorelli felt sweat beads instantly appear on her forehead. She wiped them away as Ovid looked up.

'Hello Lorelli. S'warm, isn't it,' he said.

'I'm sorry?' said Lorelli.

'It's warm,' said Ovid, tenderly holding each large leaf of one of his favourite plants and spraying it with water.

'Yes,' said Lorelli suspiciously. 'Would you mind telling me where you went after breakfast this morning?'

'Not at all. I practised a piano piece in the key of B minor. After that I came here.'

'I see,' said his sister doubtfully. 'You're saying you haven't left the house all morning.'

'Not that I recall.'

'You haven't been near the stables for example?'

'The stables? No.' Ovid shrugged. 'You see this plant. Do you know what it's called?'

'No.'

'Honey gold,' he said, continuing to spray its leaves. 'Nice name, isn't it?'

'What are you up to, Ovid Thornthwaite?' Lorelli demanded.

'I'm just looking after my plants.'

'You realise that an attempt on Adam's life would be as good as breaking the truce?'

'An attempt on Adam's life?' snorted Ovid. 'You think that boy would still be bounding about like a brainless goat had I made an attempt on his life? Why don't you just come out and say what you've got to say or buzz off?'

'That's it.' His sister stamped her feet. 'Now I know you know more than you're letting on.'

'I don't know what you mean.'

'Swarm, honey, buzz, the key of B minor,' cried Lorelli. 'You know what happened this morning, don't you? You know because you were involved.'

Ovid put his spray down. 'Involved? Involved in

what?' he asked innocently.

'The swarm of killer bees that went after Adam.'

Ovid laughed. 'OK, so maybe Hazel bumped into Adam just now then told me what happened. That doesn't mean I had anything to do with it. Besides, I'm more interested in what his father is up to than that silly boy.'

'His father is here because we called him here,' stated Lorelli.

'Yesterday I caught him crying in front of our parents' portrait. Isn't that a bit odd?'

'Well, he knew them too, didn't he?'

'I know, but he was crying.'

'Honestly, Ovid, can't you understand that not everyone is like us? You've spent so long being mistrustful and deceitful you can't see that some people are just as they seem.'

'And you've spent so much time in the company of that goody-two shoes, Adam Farthing, that you're blind to what's really going on.'

'Admit that you set the bees on Adam.'

'I'll admit to no such thing,' Ovid snorted.

'I don't know what you're up to, Ovid Thornthwaite, but I'll find out,' said Lorelli, storming out of the hothouse.

THE BOXING ROOM

Lord Royston Thornthwaite, the twins' great-grandfather, had been a brutish bully of a man who enjoyed inflicting pain on other people so much that he had built a boxing ring in one of the rooms, where he would coax local men from the village to come and fight against him, with the promise of a cash prize if they defeated him. No man ever won the money and many lost a lot more than the match. It was not uncommon for men to leave with one less ear, nose or finger than they arrived with.

Since Lord Royston had passed away in 1934, the room had barely been used, but the boxing ring remained intact. The twins themselves never used it, preferring their acts of intended violence to be more subtle, clever and carefully crafted than the ancient art of grown men hitting each other, but the morning after the argument in the library Ovid followed Mr Farthing down the corridor and watched him slip into the boxing room.

Ovid ran up a nearby staircase and found a door that led to an upper gallery, which surrounded the ring, where, in his great-grandfather's time, ladies could watch the fight without fear of getting blood on their dresses. Looking down, Ovid could see Adam Farthing, wearing a T-shirt, a pair of shorts and a set of old boxing gloves on his hands, dancing around the ring.

'Look, Father, I found these gloves hanging here. They should be in a museum, they're so old,' he said. There was a large red punchbag in the middle of the boxing ring, hanging from a heavy chain attached to the ceiling. 'Would you hold the bag for me?'

Mr Farthing climbed awkwardly through the ropes, tripping over and tumbling into the ring.

'Come on, Dad,' said Adam.

Mr Farthing stood up and put his arms uncertainly around the punchbag.

'See how hard I can hit.' Adam laid into the bag with his fists.

'Oof,' grunted Mr Farthing, looking winded by the force of his son's punch. He got his breath back and said, 'Now, son, listen to me. I wanted to say this to you somewhere private.' He looked around to check no one was listening. 'I don't want you taking any more risks. Do you understand?'

'What risks?' asked Adam cheerfully.

'The incident with the bread was too close. Please don't eat anything unless it has been prepared by one of us.'

'But that was just that stupid girl's mistake.' Adam landed more punches into the bag.

'And I heard something about an incident with some bees yesterday.'

'Oh that was nothing.'

'Thornthwaite Manor is a more dangerous place than you imagine.'

Adam stopped dancing around and looked at his father. 'What do you mean?'

Mr Farthing lowered his voice. 'I mean that those Thornthwaite twins have violent tendencies. Violent, Adam. You can't trust them.'

Adam smiled and placed an outstretched arm on his father's shoulder. 'Father, I think you underestimate the power of my charm. Lorelli likes me a great deal.'

'It's not the girl I'm worried about,' said Mr Farthing. 'It's the boy.'

'Hah! I can handle that pipsqueak, Ovid. Lorelli likes me. All I have to do is to stay on her good side and in a few years' time I'll ask her to marry me and she'll say yes because she never leaves this place, so she'll never meet anyone else. Then I'll be rich.'

'Oh, Adam, money isn't everything.' Mr Farthing shook his head. 'We have everything we need.'

'I want more than I need.'

'You're too much like your mother. Why can't you be content with what you have?'

'What do I have? Nothing. I want more.' Adam raised his gloved hands in the air. 'All this land and money is wasted on the Thornthwaite twins.'

In the gallery above, Ovid remained hidden and silent.

'Now, son, you're too bold. I knew I shouldn't have let you come with me. You must be careful. I've already lost a wife. I will not lose a son too.' Mr Farthing spoke sternly. 'The Thornthwaite twins are as deadly as poison.'

Ovid allowed himself a small smile at this description, but Adam seemed less impressed.

'I told you,' he said. 'I can handle them.' He took a couple of steps back and hit the punchbag so hard that it swung across the ring and, before his father could move out of the way, whacked into his large back, knocking him clean off his feet. The sound of Mr Farthing's face slamming into the stretched canvas echoed around the high-ceilinged room.

Ovid expected Adam to show concern and dive to his father's side, so he was surprised when, instead, Mr Farthing's son threw his head back and laughed.

THE SEVEN DANCES OF FRANCISKA TÓTH

Lorelli had lost count of how many times she had read her favourite book, *The Seven Dances of Franciska Tóth*. She knew there were lots of other books in the world that were probably more worthy of her attention, but there was something about Imelda Gaunt's novel which always drew her back.

It was a simple enough story, recounting the life of a girl called Franciska Tóth, who was born into a peasant family in nineteenth-century Hungary. For as long as she could remember, Franciska had wanted to be a dancer. Her mother and father were dismissive of her ambition, saying that dancing was not an appropriate pursuit for a girl from her humble background. They wanted her to find a good husband with some land and become a farmer's wife, like generations of her family before her.

Throughout the book, Franciska fearlessly battled

all obstacles and, with each dance she performed, drew closer to escaping the drudgery of farm life and achieving her goal of winning a place in the Hungarian State Ballet.

Lorelli loved Franciska's positive outlook on life.

However, although Lorelli adored the first hundred and seventy-four pages, she detested the last five. As the book reached its conclusion, Franciska finally got the chance to take part in an audition for the ballet but, days before it, while practising, she twisted her ankle. Compared to all the other problems she had encountered a twisted ankle was nothing and, the first time she read it, Lorelli fully expected her to overcome this problem. To her utter dismay, the last few pages of the book told of how Franciska never made the audition, and how her ankle never fully recovered. The author summed up the rest of Franciska Tóth's life in the final couple of paragraphs, saying how she never danced again, not even at her own wedding, where she married a kind-hearted pig farmer with four acres of land and thirty-six pigs.

After finishing the book for the first time Lorelli threw it across the library in frustration. A few days later she returned to pick it up and found herself opening it and looking at the first sentence.

Her whole life, Franciska Tóth only danced seven dances in public.

There it was, an indication of how the story would end in the opening sentence. Lorelli reread the book to look for other clues and found that she loved it just as much as before, in spite of the disappointment that awaited her in the final pages.

Each time she reread it, she vowed to stop before the end and yet, each time, she was unable to stop herself. She even tried writing a happier ending in which Franciska danced the audition and joined the ballet company. However, Lorelli discovered that writing a story is very different to reading one, and could never create a happy ending that worked.

THE OLD OAK TREE

Lorelli took her well-worn copy of *The Seven Dances of Franciska Tóth* to one of her favourite spots beneath the old oak tree in the south-west corner of the grounds and sat down to read.

The old oak tree had stood there for hundreds of years. Had it been able to talk it would have had some terrible stories to tell, but none was worse than the death of Lord Elroy Thornthwaite, the twins' great-great-grandfather.

Lord Elroy was a rare thing among the twins' ancestors in that he had been genuinely popular in his time. His picture in the portrait room showed a well-rounded man, with kind green eyes and reddened cheeks. He had fallen in love with and married a local village girl by the name of Eliza Tripsake. For their wedding, Lord Elroy threw a huge party at the manor for all the local villagers, with music and entertainment and plentiful food and drink.

After a couple of years, Eliza produced a baby boy, whom they named Royston. On his son's sixteenth birthday Lord Elroy decided to sell the villagers their land for a discounted price. The villagers were overjoyed because they would no longer have to spend all their hard-earned money on rent to the Thornthwaites. However, days before Lord Elroy was to sign the papers, tragedy struck. He was discovered hanging from one of the thick branches of the old oak tree. For reasons that would never be known it appeared he had taken his own life. His wife died a month later. The coroner proclaimed that Lady Thornthwaite had died from a broken heart.

Unfortunately, young Royston Thornthwaite inherited none of his father's generous spirit, so the villagers continued to pay rent for their homes and land as they still did today.

'Hello Lorelli,' said a voice.

Lorelli looked up from her book to find Adam Farthing standing in front of her, wearing a blue bicycle helmet, and gripping the handlebars of Ovid's bicycle. He dismounted and flung the bike to the ground.

'You should be more careful with other people's property,' said Lorelli.

'Oh, sorry,' replied Adam. He picked up the bike and leant it against the tree.

'Does Ovid know you're riding his bike?'

'Do you think he'll mind?'

'Definitely. Where are you going with it?'

'I thought I'd try again to visit the village but I didn't fancy giving the horses another go.'

'I see.'

'It's quite a good bike,' said Adam. 'I mean, it looks like a piece of junk but it rides really well and the suspension is fantastic.'

'Ovid takes good care of it. I don't think he'll be happy when he finds out you're riding it. You'd better not keep it out for too long. Have a nice time at the village,' said Lorelli dismissively.

'What are you reading?' enquired Adam.

'Just a book,' said Lorelli, trying to hide it.

'Can I see?'

Reluctantly Lorelli showed it to him, knowing that not to do so would only make him more curious.

'Imelda Gaunt?' said Adam. 'I know her.'

'You know her?' said Lorelli, stunned.

'She's one of my dad's clients. I've met her loads of times. I could introduce you some time, get your book signed.'

'That would be amazing. What's she like?'

'I'll tell you if you come to the village with me.'

Lorelli paused before replying. She had taken the incident with the bees as a sign that her instincts were right, that she should avoid Little Fledgling, but sitting under the old oak, with Adam Farthing standing in the dappled sunlight smiling at her, look-ing so carefree and relaxed, she changed her mind.

'All right, then. I will come.' She stood up, closed her book and placed it in her bag. She wheeled the bicycle out into the sunlight, then turned around to see Adam bending down, picking something up. 'What is it?'

'I think you've dropped some money,' replied Adam.

'I don't think so,' said Lorelli, who rarely had any need to carry money.

'Well, there's a pound coin down here,' he said, bending down to pick it up.

As he did so, there was a popping sound above him, followed by a creak. Lorelli looked up but before she could call out one of the tree's thick branches snapped and came crashing down on Adam's head. Adam Farthing crumpled to the ground.

A BOOBY-TRAPPED TREE

'Adam, Adam, are you OK?' Lorelli scrabbled to pull the branch off him. She heaved and pushed it to one side. Adam was lying still, with his eyes closed. 'Adam, say something,' she said, putting her ear to his chest to listen for a heartbeat.

She felt him move and saw him open his eyes.

'My neck really hurts,' he said.

Lorelli fought hard not to show the immense relief she felt. 'Are you able to sit up?'

Adam raised himself up on his elbows.

'It's lucky you were wearing that helmet,' she said.

Adam felt the dent in his bicycle helmet. 'I guess this old tree is a bit rotten.'

Lorelli examined where the branch had fallen from the tree. 'This oak is old, but it's still healthy,' she said. 'And look, it's a clean break.'

Adam got to his feet and saw that where the branch had fallen from the tree, there were no messy splinters as one might expect from a rotten branch. There was a perfect circle as though the branch had been sawn off. 'I wonder why it fell at that precise moment,' he said.

'Where did you find that coin?' asked Lorelli.

Still rubbing his neck, Adam helped Lorelli push the fallen branch to one side and they searched the ground for the spot where he had found the coin. With the branch gone there was less shade and Lorelli noticed something glint in the sunlight. She fell to her knees and wiped away the dirt.

'Is it more money?' asked Adam.

'No, but it is metal. Look.'

She dug into the dirt with her fingernails until she found a wire connected to the metal object. Yanking it, she found that it had been buried under a thin layer of dirt. She followed it to the tree and saw that it ran up the far side of the bark to where the branch had snapped. The wood was blackened around where the wire stopped, which was at the point where the branch had broken.

'I don't understand,' said Adam.

'The coin you found was on top of this bit of metal,' said Lorelli. 'It connected the circuit. By picking up the coin you broke the circuit and triggered a small explosion. That was the popping sound we heard. As the branch had already been half sawn off, that was all it took for it to fall.'

'Wow.' Adam took off his bicycle helmet and

scratched his head. 'But why would anyone do all that?'

'Don't you see? First the bees, now this. Someone's trying to kill you . . . or at least scare you away.'

'Me? Who would want to do such a thing to me?'

Lorelli sighed at Adam's innocence, but she didn't tell him what she was thinking. She knew exactly who would want to harm him and who would have the skill and deviousness to concoct such a plan: her twin brother, Ovid Thornthwaite.

THE END OF THE TRUCE

'I'd prefer it if you didn't tell my father about the wire,' said Adam as he and Lorelli walked back towards the manor.

'You'll have to see Nurse Griddle about your neck. What will you say happened?' Lorelli wheeled the bike alongside Adam.

'I'll tell her the truth, that a rotten branch fell and hit me.'

'But that's not the truth.'

'No,' Adam said forcefully. 'Look, Dad can be a little over-protective at times. If he thinks I'm in danger he'll send me away.'

'Maybe that would be for the best.'

Adam stopped and looked at her. 'But I really like it here. I like the manor and the grounds . . . and you. I think I'd rather be here than anywhere else.'

'Even Saint Swivels?'

'Oh, the school is great during term time but there's

no one around during the holidays and our house is in the middle of nowhere. I'd much rather stay here. Besides, we haven't even managed to make it to the village yet.'

'You should go and rest your neck. I'll send Nurse Griddle over.'

They had reached the driveway leading to the manor.

'All right, but will you promise not to tell Dad what happened?' said Adam.

'I promise.' Lorelli handed the bike to him. 'You should put this back where you found it.'

Inside Thornthwaite Manor, Lorelli found Nurse Griddle and told her about Adam's injured neck, then asked where her brother was. Nurse Griddle said she hadn't seen him all morning.

It took a while to track Ovid down. He wasn't in the music room or the hothouse or in any of his usual hideouts. Eventually it was Mrs Bagshaw who said she had seen him heading towards the barn. As she approached it, Lorelli could hear a rhythmic sound of sawing wood.

She entered and found Ovid standing with his sleeves rolled up, holding a long saw in one hand and a piece of wood in the other. Lorelli thought about the clean cut through the oak branch. Ovid seemed utterly absorbed in the activity and it was only after the piece of wood ker-clunked to the ground, that he looked up and noticed his sister.

'Hello Lorelli,' he said.

'Guess what?' she replied.

'I may need more of a clue than that.'

'Really? I would have thought that would have been enough.'

'No, I'll need a little more.' He picked up the fallen piece of wood and examined it.

'There was another attempt on Adam's life this morning. And I believe you were behind it.'

Ovid smiled. 'My dear sister,' he said, his bottle-green eyes meeting hers, 'as far as I am concerned, you are, and have always been, the only person important enough to me to warrant an attempt on your life.'

'I'm touched.'

'But you suspect me of branching out, do you?' said Ovid. 'Well, you're barking up the wrong tree.'

'You think you're so clever, but I'm on to you. I wouldn't be surprised if you told Hazel to put nuts in the bread mix too.'

'Your lack of trust is like a splinter in my heart.'

'If it wasn't you how could you possibly know what happened this morning to make those awful puns?'

'Oh, come on, nothing stays secret very long around here. Hit by a falling branch.' He chuckled. 'Even the trees don't like him.'

'You know perfectly well that it wasn't an accident,' insisted Lorelli.

'He wouldn't still be walking around with a sore neck if I was behind it.' threatened Ovid.

'I found the wire, Ovid.'

'The wire?' Ovid placed the piece of wood down and walked around to stand face to face with his sister. 'You think that if I made an attempt on Adam's life you would find a wire?'

'Well, you had better look out for wires from now on.'

'What does that mean?'

'It means the truce is off,' said Lorelli, with steely determination in her voice.

'Lorelli, think about what you're saying. Once the new will is drawn up, neither of us will benefit from the other's death.'

'The will hasn't been drawn up yet.'

'Lorelli, don't be foolish. I overheard Farthing and his son talking. Adam's plan is to marry you when you're old enough so he can get his hands on our inheritance.'

'Don't be stupid. I don't believe you.' Lorelli felt blood rush to her pale cheeks.

'Believe what you want. It's true.'

'I'm not going to marry anyone. I'm only thirteen.'

'But in a few years you will be old enough. I heard him say it. That's the only reason he's being nice to you.'

'You're just trying to turn me against him!' shouted

Lorelli. 'You're the deceitful one. You're behind these attacks.'

'Please, Lorelli, I swear I may have found Adam's accidents funny but I wasn't behind any of them. You have to believe me.'

'I should never have believed you. The alliance and the truce are both over.'

'But what about the will?' pleaded Ovid.

'That just gives us a time limit to finish the job, doesn't it?' With which Lorelli spun around, sending a cloud of sawdust behind her as she stormed out of the barn.

Stepping into the sunlight she walked straight into Mr Farthing.

'I'm sorry,' he said, dropping a file of papers on to the ground. 'I was passing when I heard raised voices. Is everything all right, Lorelli?'

Lorelli gathered herself and took a deep breath. She bent down to help Mr Farthing pick up his papers. 'Everything is fine, thank you,' she said. 'In fact everything is completely back to normal.'

ACT TWO

A DIFFERENT KIND OF GAME

The day after the argument in the barn Lorelli and Ovid sat down to continue their chess game. With barely a moment's thought Lorelli moved a knight within striking distance of Ovid's queen. Ovid raised his eyebrows and, after careful consideration, moved his queen out of danger. Lorelli instantly responded by placing it under attack again, this time from her rook. Ovid made another defensive move and Lorelli threatened the queen with a pawn.

'You're acting a little rashly,' said Ovid, considering his next move. 'You've left your bishop vulnerable.'

'You worry about your pieces, I'll worry about mine,' replied Lorelli.

'Fair enough.' Ovid took Lorelli's bishop with his rook and handed the piece to her. Lorelli placed the cold metal chess-piece next to the board.

If Lorelli was being honest with herself she would have known that the result of the game was now a foregone conclusion. It would take some time but, short of a colossal mistake by Ovid, she had lost the game. Looking at her, Ovid couldn't tell whether she had realised this or not.

The silence that hung between them was broken by Adam Farthing entering the room, sporting a pair of dazzling white tennis shorts and holding two wooden tennis rackets.

'Morning Ovid,' he said cheerfully. 'Hello Lorelli, are you ready for our match?' He waved the rackets in the air.

'What match?' said Ovid.

'Tennis, of course.' Adam grinned.

'Tennis?' Ovid sounded as revolted as if Adam had suggested that they spend the morning throwing cowpats at each other.

'Yes, I have a world-class coach at Saint Swivels. He used to rank eighteenth in the world. These rackets are a bit old-fashioned but I think they'll still work.'

Lorelli took one of the rackets from Adam. 'This was Mother's,' she said, turning it over in her hand. 'Our parents used to play together.'

'How would you know?' said Ovid incredulously. 'You don't remember them any more than I do.'

'You don't know what I remember,' replied Lorelli. 'Besides, Tom told me they used to play together when they first got married.'

'And now you and Adam are going to play with

their rackets,' said Ovid. 'How romantic.'

'Come on, Adam,' said Lorelli. 'Let's go. Ovid only hates tennis because he can't beat me at it.'

'Unlike chess,' said Ovid under his breath.

'See you later, Ovid,' said Adam cheerfully.

They left the room and Ovid remained at the chessboard, working out what moves would most quickly put his sister out of her misery and end the game.

'Good morning young master,' said Mr Crutcher, entering, carrying a tray. 'Will you not be joining the others on the tennis court?'

'No, I can't bear the stupid game.'

Mr Crutcher smiled. 'Of course not. You take after Lord Thornthwaite in that way.'

'Lorelli said he used to play with Mother.'

Mr Crutcher set about clearing the empty teacups from the table. 'Your father tolerated the game for your mother's sake.'

'Alfred,' said Ovid.

'Yes, young master?'

'Do you really think Mother killed Father for the money?'

Mr Crutcher paused in what he was doing. 'I'm afraid I do, young master. Greed can make people do terrible things.'

A LOOSE WHEEL

The previous summer the twins had played a few games of tennis together but it soon became apparent that Lorelli was naturally more talented at the sport than her brother. Ovid didn't like losing. The first tennis match he lost was the last he ever played.

In fact, the only outdoor pursuit that Ovid really enjoyed was cycling. A few years ago he had come across an old mountain bike, rusty and falling apart. Its seat was threadbare and jammed with rust. Both pedals had snapped off, several spokes were missing from the wheels and the tyres were flat.

Ovid had delved into books in the library on bicycle maintenance, welding, DIY and anything else that could help him restore the bike. He became so utterly engrossed that he didn't try to kill his sister for several weeks, although a deadly viper in his bed suggested that Lorelli hadn't given up her murderous ambitions.

Tom Paine gave him something to sort out the rust

and Mr Crutcher ordered the parts required to fix it, but apart from that Ovid repaired the bike entirely on his own. Eventually, with new pedals, a fresh paintjob, working wheels and pumped-up tyres, his bike was ready. The next challenge he faced was learning how to ride it.

Most children have parents to help them learn to ride a bicycle. Many start with tricycles or stabilisers to build up their confidence. Not Ovid. In spite of an offer from Tom to teach him, Ovid took the bicycle around the back of the manor and set about learning how to ride on his own. He fell a number of times. Nurse Griddle got used to tending to his grazed hands and knees but eventually, through sheer determination, he succeeded in teaching himself.

He loved to take his bike out for long rides. Sometimes he even got as far as Beryl's Bridge but he always stopped short of the village.

Today, he didn't want to head south, past the tennis courts, so he turned his bike north up Orwell Hill, where he could amuse himself freewheeling down the slopes.

There was something strange about the feel of the bike today. Ovid wondered whether someone else had ridden it and, riding over the crunching gravel, past the old barn up into Huxley Woods, he noticed that a sweet smell seemed to be following him.

He grew breathless as the gradient grew steeper.

Once he had gained enough height he turned around and glided down the hill, through the woods. He gained speed as he dodged trees. As usual, he enjoyed the danger but when he felt himself going too fast he eased on the brakes. He expected the brakes to squeal as the bike slowed but there was no noise. He squeezed harder but still nothing happened. The bike was picking up speed, the handlebars vibrating violently against his palms. He turned to the left, trying to head back up the slope to slow the bike down but doing so, he felt a sharp, sudden jolt. The front wheel came loose and rolled away, tipping the bike and flipping him over the handlebars. The rest of the bike went flying over his head and he crashed head first into the middle of a thorny bush.

After the noise and chaos of the crash, lying in the middle of the bush, looking up at the blue sky, he felt strangely peaceful.

'Ouch,' he muttered, feeling the pain of hundreds of thorns digging into him. He tried to extract himself from the bush but with every movement more thorns penetrated his skin. He attempted to stand but as he put weight on his right foot he felt it give way and an agonising pang of pain shoot from his heel. Struggling out of the bush, he tripped and landed face down. He rolled over and looked at his palms. He couldn't tell how much of the thick red liquid they were covered in was berry juice and how much was blood.

Ovid hadn't experienced such pain since Lorelli had added sulphuric acid to his bubble bath. He pulled out the thorns from his hand with his teeth but was still unable to put any weight on his right foot. When he tried crawling, every knock to his foot was agony. He raised his leg in the air and found a way of hitching himself forward on his elbows and one knee, over the muddy ground to the remains of his bike.

The back wheel was badly bent out of shape and the front had rolled out of sight. Had the bike been in better condition he might have been able to lean on it to get himself back to the manor. As it was, it was useless to him.

The brake cord had been cut. He cursed himself for not noticing it before. He turned his attention to the front wheel. Tiny scratches around the paintwork indicated that someone had loosened the bolt that held the wheel in place.

'Lorelli,' he said, but something about it bothered him. His sister's schemes, like his own, tended to be better thought out than this. A loose wheel and a cut brake were likely to cause an accident but were highly unlikely to cause his death.

Once again, he noticed the sweet smell. It seemed to be coming from his bike. He sniffed, trying to locate the source, and discovered that the smell was stronger around the saddle. He undid the bolt that held it down, yanked it off and lowered a finger into the connecting tube. There was something moist and squishy inside. He retrieved his finger and saw that it was covered in a gold-coloured gooey substance. He raised his finger to his mouth and stuck out his tongue to taste it. It tasted sweet, rich and spicy.

'Honey? Why would she put honey inside the bike tubes?' he wondered out loud.

Then the answer to his question stepped into sight. Standing on all fours, a couple of metres in front of him, was a large, brown bear. It looked at Ovid and snorted, its nostrils flaring out as it did so. Ovid froze. The bear tipped back on to its hind legs, let out a low growl and fell back down, beating the ground with its forepaws.

WHAT TO DO IF FACED WITH A LARGE BROWN BEAR

Ovid had once read a book on bears, which began like this:

> The popularity of the teddy bear among small children has led many to believe that bears are sweet and cuddly. This is wrong. Bears are large, muscular, wild creatures that will tear you limb from limb as soon as look at you.

The book went on to list bears as one of the most dangerous animals in the world. It also stated that, whereas bears are common in parts of America and Canada, there are no wild bears in the UK.

Faced with the current evidence, Ovid was reminded that you couldn't believe everything you read in books. However, since it was his only frame of reference he tried to remember what other advice the book had given. He recalled it mentioning that in the event of coming face to face with an angry bear, the best thing to do was to avoid eye contact, speak calmly and slowly retreat.

With his foot still hurting, Ovid was unable to retreat, so he lowered his gaze and spoke in a low, calm voice.

'My name is Ovid Thornthwaite. I mean you no harm,' he said, feeling a little silly. 'I was out cycling when my bicycle broke and I came off it and landed in that bush.' He pointed to the bush but kept his eyes on the ground. 'I know you can't understand me but . . .'

His concentration was broken by a strange sensation on his outstretched finger. He glanced up and saw that the bear was licking the honey off it. Ovid quickly lowered his eyes, not wanting to anger the animal while its teeth were so close to his finger.

'There's more inside the bike,' said Ovid, moving his finger gradually to the bike tube. The bear followed it down and sniffed the honey-filled tube, quickly losing interest in Ovid's finger and licking the inside of the bike tube with its long tongue instead.

Careful not to make a sudden movement Ovid slowly brought his finger away and watched as the bear's long tongue finished off the honey. Still unable to get away, he hoped that the bear would lose interest in him once the honey was finished, but as it retrieved less and less with each lick, the huge beast growled. It was still hungry. With the honey finished it turned its attention back to Ovid. It reared up then fell down on the bike, bending the frame.

Keeping his eyes lowered Ovid found a stick with his right hand and picked it up. The final thing the book had to say on the subject of surviving a bear attack was this:

> Do not play dead. If you do this, you soon won't be playing. The best way to survive a bear attack, if you have no other choice, is to fight back, preferably while shouting. In certain circumstances this has been known to scare a bear away but since the bear is likely to be bigger, stronger and faster than you, good luck.

Ovid took a deep breath and screamed, 'GO AWAY AND BOTHER SOMEONE ELSE, YOU STUPID BEAR,' while whacking the stick against the animal's nose.

The bear looked genuinely surprised by this sudden change in tactic and to his immense relief it turned and fled into the woods.

HOW TO SERVE

Adam Farthing had the strangest tennis technique Lorelli had ever seen. His serve involved throwing the ball high in the air, waiting until it was virtually shoulder height, then leaping back and whacking it, more often than not sending it straight into the net, and yet Adam didn't seem concerned about his shortcomings.

After his first double fault, he smiled and said, 'I guess, that's one nil to you.'

'It's fifteen love,' replied Lorelli.

'Fifteen for that one shot?'

'That's how the scores work in tennis: fifteen, thirty, forty, game.' Lorelli was unsure whether he was joking.

'Oh yes, silly me.' Adam picked up the ball to serve again. 'I'm getting it mixed up with squash.'

With his next serve he did manage to get a ball over the net. Lorelli sent the ball back to the left side of the court and watched as Adam ran across in an attempt to get the shot with his forehand.

'It would have been easier to play with your back-hand.'

'My what hand?' asked Adam.

Lorelli showed him.

'Oh yes, that would have been easier,' said Adam. 'Is it my serve again?'

By the end of the first set he had only managed to win a couple of points, both from what Lorelli considered to be lucky shots.

'Let's have a break,' said Lorelli, seeing Hazel approaching.

'I'm not tired at all,' said Adam cheerfully.

Hazel was carrying a tray with two glasses of fresh lemonade. 'I thought you might be thirsty,' she said.

Adam scowled at her. 'No nuts in there, are there?'

Hazel lowered her gaze and muttered an apology.

'Well then.' Adam picked up a glass, took a sip then pulled a face. 'It's a bit bitter.'

'Mrs Bagshaw doesn't put much sugar in,' said Lorelli, taking her glass. 'Thank you, Hazel.'

'You're welcome.'

'It wasn't her fault, you know,' said Lorelli to Adam after Hazel had left. 'Poor Hazel. Mrs Bagshaw is vey strict with her, making her work as a maid.'

'At least she has a mother.'

'Actually, she's adopted. Her real mother aban-doned her. Besides, you should be grateful. You've still got your father.'

'Him? Oh he's useless. I mean, you'd think a lawyer would make good money, wouldn't you?'

'He earns enough to send you to Saint Swivels.'

'Barely,' snorted Adam. 'Come on, let's play another game. I really think I'm going to win a game this time. Or at least get as far as truce.'

'Deuce,' corrected Lorelli.

'That's the one. Is it my turn to serve?' replied Adam.

THE HAUNTING MELODY

Ovid was beginning to lose heart. He had been shouting for help for the best part of an hour. He felt thwarted. He felt foolish. How could he have been so careless as to not check that the bike hadn't been tampered with? He had let his guard down and Lorelli had taken advantage. He was in no doubt that this was her handiwork. He allowed himself a moment of admiration for his sister's cunning. Acquiring a bear couldn't have been easy.

But now he needed to get home so he was relieved to hear someone nearby whistling a mournful melody.

'Hello?' he shouted.

The whistling stopped.

'Who's that?' replied Tom Paine, the gardener.

'It's me, Ovid,' he replied. 'I've hurt my foot.'

'Keep talking,' said Tom. 'I'll follow your voice.'

Ovid started telling Tom how he had fallen off his bike and hurt his foot, leaving out any mention of the bear or his suspicion that his sister was behind the attack.

'Not a fun morning, then,' said Tom, appearing from behind a tree, pushing a wheelbarrow full of cut flowers.

Ovid smiled at the sight of the old man. 'It's good to see you, Tom. Could you help get me home?'

'Not a problem.' Tom tipped the flowers out of the wheelbarrow and bent down to pick up Ovid, who winced in pain as his bad ankle banged against the side of it. 'Sorry, Master Ovid,' said Tom, placing him inside.

Ovid felt uncomfortable and he had to place an arm behind his head to stop it banging against the metal but he was grateful to be getting out of his predicament.

As he made his way towards the manor, Tom resumed his whistling. It was a strange tune that only seemed to consist of eight or nine notes before repeating.

'What is that?' asked Ovid.

'Sorry,' replied Tom. 'A bad habit of mine, whistling, I'm afraid, sir. I spend so much time on my own I don't even notice I'm doing it.'

'Yes, but what's the tune?'

'Let me see.' Tom whistled a few bars of it again, trying to identify it. 'Oh, do you know, I think it was one of your mother's.'

'What do you mean, one of my mother's?' said Ovid.

'One of the tunes she wrote.'

'I knew she played the piano. I never knew she composed.'

'Oh yes,' said Tom. 'Lovely little melodies. Never had no words though. I think you need words too, don't you?'

'Did she write them down?'

'I'm not too sure,' said Tom, 'but I do remember her playing this one just before she passed away.'

Tom began to whistle again and Ovid wondered what it said about a woman who could write such a strange and haunting tune. He knew so little about his parents.

WHERE THERE'S BLAME

Tom parked the wheelbarrow outside the servants' entrance. 'I'll pop in and get Nurse Griddle,' he said.

'Thank you, Tom,' said Ovid, surprised that Nurse Griddle's sixth sense for injury hadn't already brought her to the door. He hoped that Tom would find her quickly. He didn't want Lorelli or Adam to find him in this vulnerable state. Growing up in Thornthwaite Manor had taught him to avoid being seen when one was at one's weakest.

Although he felt certain that Lorelli was behind this latest attempt on his life, he still had to keep an eye on Mr Farthing and Adam. Their presence in Thornthwaite Manor had shifted the delicate balance of life there. Ovid missed having the clarity of a singular enemy in the form of his sister. The idea that there might be more than one now concerned him deeply.

He felt something land on his stomach and saw Cowell, Lorelli's cat. Ovid didn't particularly like animals, but at this moment of uncertainty he found something comforting and reassuring about Cowell's purring. At least she was trustworthy.

'Hello Ovid. What are you doing in a wheelbarrow?' said a voice behind him.

Ovid craned his head around to see Mr Farthing peering down at him, clutching his leather bag to his chest. Startled, Cowell jumped off and scurried away.

'I've hurt my foot,' said Ovid as the large lawyer rounded the wheelbarrow and came face to face with him.

'And your head,' said Mr Farthing, adjusting his spectacles.

Ovid reached a hand to his forehead. He looked at it and saw blood.

'Tripped over playing, did you?' said Mr Farthing.

'The wheel came off my bicycle,' replied Ovid simply.

'Statistically speaking, cycling is more dangerous than parachuting,' said the lawyer.

'I'll stick to parachuting from now on, then,' said Ovid sarcastically.

Mr Farthing laughed nervously. 'No, no, no. I simply mean that the activities that seem safe are often the most dangerous . . . statistically, that is. As a lawyer I often find that. I'd be more than happy to inspect your bicycle. You may be able to sue the manufacturer for faulty goods. Where there's blame, there's a claim and all that . . .'

'You think the manufacturer filled the tubes with honey in order to provoke a large brown bear to attack me?' said Ovid, watching Mr Farthing closely for a reaction.

Mr Farthing laughed again. 'What imagination you children have. Imagine that, a bear in these woods.'

'Imagine,' said Ovid drily.

'Should I fetch Nurse Griddle?' said Mr Farthing.

'Nurse Griddle is away for a couple of days.' said Mr Crutcher, appearing at the door.

'Where is she?' asked Ovid.

'She's away dealing with some family business. I'll take you to see Doctor Scragg.' He lifted the wheelbarrow by the handles and wheeled Ovid towards the car, leaving Mr Farthing behind.

'Who's Doctor Scragg?'

Mr Crutcher opened the car door and lifted Ovid out of the wheelbarrow.

'He's the village doctor.'

DOCTOR SCRAGG

Considering the number of close brushes with death Ovid had experienced in his thirteen years, it was surprising that he had never visited the village doctor but, until now, Nurse Griddle had been available and able to deal with every cut, bruise, graze and occasional bullet wound which the twins had inflicted on each other.

Ovid sat beside Mr Crutcher, looking nervously around the waiting room, reading the posters on the walls about various illnesses and ways to prevent them. He felt uncomfortable being in the village. On the way there, he had lowered himself in the car seat for fear of being seen. He knew that his fear was irrational. He understood that the village wasn't full of rampaging hordes looking to burn down Thornthwaite Manor, but he also knew from Mr Crutcher's local history lessons how, with a few exceptions, his ancestors had not been kind to the villagers.

The door opened and an elderly man in a three-piece suit pushed a wheelchair into the room. He had wiry grey hair and a well-lined face, which folded naturally into a warm smile.

'Hello, Alfred, it's been a while,' said Doctor Scragg.

'Thirteen years, Donald,' replied Mr Crutcher.

'That long? And this must be Ovid.' Doctor Scragg looked at him. 'You look just like your father. Do you need a hand getting into this wheelchair?'

'No.' Ovid lifted himself into the wheelchair, before Mr Crutcher could help him. 'Did you know my father?'

'Oh yes, we were childhood friends. Now let's get you into my surgery.' Doctor Scragg wheeled Ovid towards the door. Mr Crutcher held the door open for them. 'Thank you, Alfred,' said Doctor Scragg.

Mr Crutcher began to follow them but the doctor said, 'If you don't mind, I prefer to see my patients alone.'

'Of course. I'll be right here should you need me, young master.' Mr Crutcher closed the door behind them.

Doctor Scragg pushed Ovid up to the desk and then took his place behind it. 'An excellent butler but a little overprotective at times, don't you find?' he said, taking a pen and writing something down.

'Mr Crutcher has been very kind to me and my sister,' replied Ovid.

'Ah, your sister. Lorelli, isn't it?'

'Yes.'

'You don't have a middle name, do you?'

'No,' said Ovid, leaning forward to see what he was writing.

'This is your medical card.' Doctor Scragg showed him. 'The last time I wrote your name was on your birth certificate.'

'My birth certificate?'

'I remember that day very well. There was all that fuss about your sister being the first ever girl born into the family. Your father seemed most distressed but your mother was very calm about it, considering how much she had been through to bring you both into the world. Now, let's have a look at this foot of yours.'

Doctor Scragg took off Ovid's sock and examined his foot, gently squeezing it.

'Is it broken?' asked Ovid, wincing.

'No. It's sprained.'

'How long will it take to get better?'

'A couple of days and it should be on the mend. I'll give you some crutches until then. Now, let me have a look at that cut on your head.'

As the doctor disinfected the cut on Ovid's head, Ovid asked, 'Will it turn into a scar like my fathers?'

'Your father's scar? Yes, that was an odd thing. I was there the night he got it.'

'You were hunting with him?'

'Hunting? Goodness, no. He got that scar after a collision with a waiter carrying a breadknife.' Doctor Scragg scratched his chin.

'A breadknife?'

'That's right. It was the night after you were born. We were having dinner together. He went to the toilet and when he came back he was holding his head. That's how he got the scar.'

'Alfred must have been mistaken,' said Ovid.

'Perhaps he was trying to make it sound more glamorous,' said Doctor Scragg, wheeling Ovid out of the surgery back into the waiting room.

Mr Crutcher was standing with his back to the room, looking out of the window. He turned around and said, 'Home, young master?'

'Yes, please,' replied Ovid.

Keeping his head down again to avoid being seen, Ovid didn't notice his sister and Adam Farthing walking in the opposite direction.

FATHER WHELAN

Lorelli was too concerned about being recognised by the villagers herself to notice Ovid drive past. She had never intended to come so far but, during their walk, she had been so engrossed in conversation with Adam that she failed to notice when they reached the bridge that crossed the River Curtail at the edge of the village.

'What's Imelda Gaunt like?' Lorelli asked as they walked.

'She looks a bit like you,' Adam said thoughtfully. 'She's very beautiful,' he added, making Lorelli blush, 'and really intelligent.'

'Has she written anything else?'

'She doesn't need to. That book has made her loads of money.'

'Really? Is it popular?' Lorelli felt a pang of jealousy. She had liked the feeling that the story belonged to her alone.

'Oh yes. I should say she was a millionaire probably.'

'But she didn't write it for the money, surely?'

'Why else would you write a book? Why else would you do anything? It's all about money in the end, isn't it?'

'Can you really introduce me to her?' asked Lorelli, not wanting to dwell on this point.

'Of course.'

When they reached the outskirts of Little Fledgling, Lorelli suggested heading back but Adam said that since they had come so far they may as well go and see the village. 'We can catch the bus back,' he said. 'There's a bus stop right near Thornthwaite Manor.'

'Will it let me on?' Lorelli had never travelled by bus. The idea of it unsettled her.

Adam laughed. 'Buses let everyone on. You just stick out your hand, pay the driver your money and get on.'

'I haven't got any money,' said Lorelli.

'I can lend you some. I'm sure you'll be able to pay me back some time. I'll buy you an ice cream too.' Adam made it sound so harmless and so normal that Lorelli couldn't think of any reason to say no even though the village scared her.

They passed a man pushing a large noisy lawn-mower in front of his thatched cottage. Seeing the sharp blades rotating, chewing up the grass, Lorelli felt the urge to turn and run, but the man smiled and waved. Next door, an elderly lady was clipping her hedge. Lorelli looked fearfully at the pair of secateurs in her hand, but the old lady said, 'Good afternoon,' and went back to cutting her hedge without a second glance.

They stopped outside a tiny police station, barely bigger than the public toilet.

'You see,' said Adam, 'there's nothing to fear. Little Fledgling is a charming village.'

Lorelli looked at his grinning face and allowed herself a small sigh of relief. She relaxed. Adam was right. Everything was fine. It was a beautiful day and Little Fledgling was a quaint place full of nice people minding their own business, none of whom wanted to harm her.

But this feeling suddenly passed when a voice growled in her ear, 'You're a Thornthwaite.' A hand landed so heavily on her shoulder that she felt her legs buckle with the force.

She turned to see a man dressed entirely in black, except for a white dog collar. His lack of hair revealed an uneven skull with thin patchy skin stretched over the top. He had crooked teeth and wild eyes that darted around in their sockets before settling on her.

'Get off me,' said Lorelli, trying unsuccessfully to knock his arm away.

'You are a Thornthwaite,' he said again. His breath stank.

'So what if she is? Who are you?' demanded Adam.

The man kept his eyes trained on Lorelli. 'My name is Father Whelan. Your parents tied their terrible union in my church. Their sinful bodies lie in my graveyard. I pray that you have not inherited the sin that runs in your family.'

'What sin?' said Lorelli, trying to wrestle free.

'Murder runs through Thornthwaite blood like a virus,' said the priest, tightening his grip.

'Come on, Lorelli,' said Adam. 'Let's go.'

At last, Lorelli wriggled free but Father Whelan jumped in front of her, his black robe flapping like a giant bat. 'Murder is the deadliest sin!' he shouted, waving his arms in the air dramatically. 'Renounce it! Renounce it!'

'Leave her alone,' said Adam. 'Can't you see you're scaring her?'

'I don't know what you're talking about,' said Lorelli to the priest.

Father Whelan lunged forward and grabbed her shoulders once more, pulling her near and whispering in her ear, 'Everyone knows how your mother murdered your father. And I know what your father did before that. He was guilty of the same. He murdered a man, an innocent man, a good man.'

'What man?' said Lorelli.

'Hedley Bagshaw,' he whispered. 'The police wouldn't believe me.' He pointed across the road at the tiny police station. 'They said he was out of the country at the time. Your father probably paid them off. But I know what I saw. With my own eyes I saw him leave the printing press. There was a woman with him too. At the time, I didn't know what they had done, but when I heard what had happened to poor Hedley, then I realised. It was your father who killed him. Both your parents were murderers. You must not go down the same path.'

Lorelli knocked the priest's hands away and ran.

THEIR PARENTS' ROOM

On the drive back to Thornthwaite Manor, Ovid did not mention what Doctor Scragg had said about the scar. Once they were home, Mr Crutcher stopped the car and jumped out. He held Ovid's door open and handed him his crutches.

'Thank you, Alfred,' said Ovid. 'I can make it from here on my own.'

'Very good, young master,' said Mr Crutcher. 'I'll take the car around the back, then.'

Ovid made his way up the stairs, into the hallway. His foot was already feeling a bit better and he found it easier to walk with one crutch. He climbed the stairs and found Hazel sitting in the bay window, reading a letter.

'Have you hurt your foot?' she asked.

'I've sprained my ankle,' replied Ovid. 'Who have you got a letter from?'

'It's from my mum.'

'Why does Mrs Bagshaw write you letters?'

'Not Mrs Bagshaw. It's from my real mum.'

'The one who left you on Mrs Bagshaw's doorstep? I never knew you kept in touch.'

'She writes sometimes. She never signs them or tells me where she lives and they always get mailed from different places, so I can't write back.'

'What does she say in the letters?'

'Sorry, sir. It's private.'

'I see. Have you seen Lorelli?'

'She went for a walk with Adam after their game of tennis.'

Ovid let out a short burst of derisive laughter. 'Hah. Were they holding hands?'

'I don't think so.'

Ovid left her and hobbled down the east wing of the manor. When he reached a white door with purple flowers painted around its border, he stopped. He took the doorknob in his hand but paused before turning it. This had been his parents' room. He had been inside once before, several years ago, hoping to find some clue about why his mother had killed his father, but had discovered nothing.

But the conversation with Doctor Scragg had got him thinking about his father's scar. Either the doctor was mistaken or Mr Crutcher was confused. Or one of them was lying. Ovid knew that his ancestors were highly superstitious about having their picture taken but he had to wonder, was it possible for a man to live his entire life without being photographed?

Once inside the dark room, he flicked the light switch but the bulb had gone. He made his way around the bed and drew the curtains. Sunlight spilt in, illuminating the dust particles that Ovid had disturbed. Nothing had been touched in the room since his mother's death. On an ornate dressing table was a hairbrush with fine black strands of hair, various items of make-up and a glass, stained with a water mark where its contents had evaporated over time.

On the bedside table was a framed photograph of two people with their arms around each other. Both wore old-fashioned masks to cover their faces. Noticing a gondola in the background, Ovid remembered Mrs Bagshaw saying that his parents had honeymooned in Venice, but with the masks covering their faces Ovid could only make out his father's green eyes.

He opened the drawers but was unable to find any more photos. On the other bedside table was a book with a pair of reading glasses on top. Ovid read the title, The Seven Dances of Franciska Tóth. He had never heard of it, nor its author, Imelda Gaunt. He turned it over to read the back and a piece of paper fluttered down to the bed. Intrigued about what his mother had used for a bookmark, he picked it up. One side was blank but on the other, scribbled in blue biro, were two bars of music. There was no bass clef for the second hand and no flats or sharps in the stave. It was a simple melody that began on F and ended on D.

Wanting to hear the tune, Ovid tucked the piece of paper into his back pocket and left the room.

A TRAIN PULLS IN

'Don't worry about what that priest said. He's just a crazy old man,' said Adam.

Lorelli didn't speak. Hard as she tried she couldn't shake Father Whelan's words from her head. Both her parents were murderers, he had said. *Murder runs through Thornthwaite blood like a virus.* She had always thought the family inheritance was Thornthwaite Manor and its contents. Was it possible to inherit the tendency to murder? Was that why she and Ovid had spent their childhood trying to kill each other? Was it in their blood? She wondered. Were they born killers?

Walking down the main street of the village, it was still as beautiful a day, only now the blue sky felt almost blinding in its intensity. Lorelli could hear Adam talking, trying to sound chirpy and light, but she wasn't listening. She felt like every villager that passed her looked at her accusingly: a postman delivering post, a teenage girl walking a dog, a mother pushing a child in a pushchair. *Everyone knows*, the priest had said. What were these people thinking as they glanced at her then quickly looked away? She was so obviously a Thornthwaite with her black hair and green eyes. Did they all know the terrible truth of her parents' deaths?

'I said, what flavour do you want?'

Adam was standing in front of her. They had stopped outside the village shop.

'Flavour?' said Lorelli vaguely.

'Ice cream,' said Adam, pointing to a sign outside the shop.

Lorelli smiled. No matter how dark her thoughts got it seemed that Adam Farthing could always remind her of normal happy things in life like ice cream.

'Vanilla?' she said, which was the only flavour that had ever been served in Thornthwaite Manor.

'Bor-ring,' sang Adam. 'I tell you what, I'll surprise you. Wait here.'

A bell tinkled as he went inside the shop. Lorelli sat down on a bench outside.

She heard a rattling, rumbling noise. Across the road was a train station where a train was pulling in. It was the first that Lorelli had ever seen.

She felt a strange urge to run across the road, jump on the train and escape her life. She remembered the passage of her favourite book in which Franciska first travelled on a train, feeling free and grown up. Lorelli wanted to feel like that. However, she remained where she was and watched the passengers walk out of the station, shielding their eyes from the sunlight. In among the strangers she saw a face she knew: Nurse Griddle. Lorelli looked down to avoid being recognised. When she looked up, Nurse Griddle had gone.

'I got you two scoops, one chocolate, one toffee,' said Adam, thrusting a large ice cream under Lorelli's nose.

'Thank you,' she said, taking it.

'What do you want to do now?'

'I want to go to the graveyard to see my parents' grave,' Lorelli replied.

MARTHA THORNTHWAITE'S MELODY

Ovid picked up the book, slipped the piece of paper between its pages and left the room with it tucked under his arm. Going downstairs with the crutch was trickier than going up, but it wasn't long before he was trying the door to the drawing room, where the piano was kept. It was locked.

'Who's in there?' he said.

No one replied. Ovid turned and headed along the east wing, until he reached the door labelled *The Organ Room*. He opened it and stepped into the high-ceilinged room.

Before him a row of huge pipes of varying sizes stood against the wall. At their base was a keyboard and red-cushioned seat. In front of the magnificent organ were several rows of wooden benches.

The *step-tap* sound of foot and crutch echoed around the room as Ovid made his way down the aisle to the organ. He sat on the cushioned stool and pulled out the piece of music. He placed it in front of him and found the first note on the keyboard.

Slowly he played the tune. Each note reverberated around the walls. It was the same tune that he had heard Tom whistle, the tune his mother wrote shortly before she died. On the organ it sounded even more haunting. He played it again, only quicker. Then once more, even faster. He hit a wrong note and began again. He tried it on the high notes, then down on the lowest octave. He played it with both hands. He wondered what his mother had been thinking when she wrote it. It sounded so angry, so dark. It felt like an incomplete sentence. He tried to work out what she had intended to come next but couldn't come up with anything good. He played it again, keeping his fingers down on each note he played, slowly creating a heavy, jarring chord that drowned the room in noise.

When he released his fingers, he heard a small cough behind him. He turned around to see Mr Farthing standing at the far end of the room.

'That's an interesting little ditty,' said the lawyer, smiling.

'What do you want?' snapped Ovid, angry at the interruption. 'Have you come to count how many pipes are on the organ?'

'Oh no,' said Mr Farthing. 'You see the organ counts as one object, irrespective of the number of pipes.'

'It was a joke,' said Ovid drily.

'Oh, I see. Yes, of course.'

'So why are you here?'

'I was passing when I heard music. It's a magnificent instrument. Eighteenth century, if I'm not mistaken.'

'Yes,' replied Ovid. The room dated back to the late eighteenth century when Lord Allegro Thornthwaite would invite nobility from all over the country to come and listen to his recitals. 'I daresay it will go down in your inventory.'

'I haven't even started on this wing of the house. You do have a lot of rooms.'

'Well, I'm leaving now, if you want to make a start.' Ovid tucked his mother's tune into his pocket and started to leave but Mr Farthing stepped in front of him, blocking his way.

'Do you want something?' asked Ovid.

'Well, yes, there was something else. A question.'

'Well?'

'Yes... I wondered if you'd be kind enough to confirm how many pets you have.'

'Pets?'

'Pets... Well, animals. How many animals are there in Thornthwaite Manor?'

'Why, are you putting them on the inventory too?'

'Everything has to be accounted for.'

'There's Cowell the cat and the two horses, Pride

and Joy.'

'So no other animals?'

'Well, Tom has his bees but they belong to him. Why do you ask?'

'It's nothing really, I mean, well, that is . . . It's just that I came across some rather peculiar documents in your sister's room.'

'What were you doing in Lorelli's room?'

'I have to itemise everything in the manor.'

'What were these documents, then?' asked Ovid sceptically.

Mr Farthing shifted uncomfortably. 'It's paperwork regarding the acquisition of an animal from a closed-down zoo. They detail the purchasing of one female of the species referred to as *Ursus arctos*.'

'What does that mean?'

'I looked it up. It's Latin. It's the name for a . . . well . . .' Mr Farthing laughed awkwardly. 'It's a type of bear.' He met Ovid's gaze. 'You were joking when you said about the bear in the woods, weren't you?'

THE LADY WITH THE FLOWERS

On their way to the graveyard, Lorelli and Adam passed the village school. It was a small modern one-storey building, surrounded by a playground, with brightly coloured patterns on the concrete that would have been filled with children playing during term time.

'What's it like?' asked Lorelli.

'I don't know, I've never been there,' said Adam.

'I mean, what's it like going to school. I've only ever been taught at home?'

'Oh that. It's great fun. Saint Swivels is much bigger than this little school, of course. It's got four football fields, eight basketball courts, twenty tennis courts, a science lab, a gym, and an Olympic-sized swimming pool. It's even got a working farm on site.'

'You sound like a brochure,' said Lorelli. 'What I mean is, what's it like having friends, going to classes, being away from home, having teachers you like and ones you don't... things like that?' She was thinking of the various books she had read about school life.

'Oh, that's all brilliant,' said Adam with a dismissive wave of his hand. 'I've got loads of friends and all the teachers like me.'

They approached the tall spire of the church. On the other side of the road from it was a flat-roofed building with a sign outside which said: *PRINTING PRESS*.

Lorelli pointed to the large wooden doors at the front of the church. 'You don't think Father Whelan's in there, do you?' she said anxiously.

'No. He walked off in the other direction,' said Adam. 'Where's your parents' grave?'

'I don't know. This is my first time here,' admitted Lorelli.

'It'll be quicker to find it if we split up to look,' said Adam brightly. 'I'll head this way around the church, you go that way.'

Lorelli agreed. She wasn't sure if she wanted Adam there when she found her parents' grave, not knowing how she would feel when she saw it.

Walking alone through the graveyard, Lorelli found it an oddly unemotional experience to read the names, dates and inscriptions of people she had never known. Then she saw a name she did recognise.

Hedley Bagshaw
Now part of the local history he loved so much
Died aged 41, 1996

'Here, my dear. Place this on his grave.'

Lorelli turned to face the woman who had spoken. She had kind eyes, long unkempt hair and several layers of mismatched clothes as though she had been unsure what to put on that morning and so had worn everything. In her arms she carried a bunch of colourful flowers, one of which she was holding out for Lorelli.

Lorelli took the flower and put it on the gravestone. 'Did you know him?' she asked.

The woman read the name on the gravestone. 'Hedley Bagshaw? No, but I come here to put flowers on the gravestones of those neglected by the living. Even the dead need caring for, don't you think?'

'I'm looking for my parents,' said Lorelli.

'Where did you last see them?'

'I mean, they're dead. I'm looking for the gravestone.'

'Oh, I'm sorry.' The woman smiled kindly. 'What name, my love?'

'Thornthwaite,' replied Lorelli, nervous about revealing her name.

She wondered whether the woman was checking her eye colour but all she said was, 'Your ancestors are in the far corner. I'll show you.'

She followed her across the graveyard. 'My name is Miss Wilde,' said the woman. 'I work in the village library. Do you read much?'

'A fair amount.' Lorelli felt a rush of excitement at the thought of a different library to explore.

'You should come and join.'

'Am I allowed? Mr Crutcher says there's no point reading other books until I've read all the ones at home.'

'Well, Mr Crutcher doesn't know what he's talking about, then. You should come to the library and have a look at our collection.'

'I will,' promised Lorelli, thinking about the possibility of finding another book by Imelda Gaunt.

Miss Wilde led her to a part of the graveyard where the grass had grown long and dandelions and buttercups had been allowed to spread. The gravestones seemed much older and many had given way to subsidence. 'This is where your family lies,' she said.

With the overhanging trees it was darker than the rest of the graveyard. Many of the gravestones were carved into elaborate shapes to signify her ancestors' passions in life. A carved globe stood on Lord Orinoco Thornthwaite's grave; on Lord Royston's was a stone boxing glove; and Lord Elroy Thornthwaite's bore a heart engraved with his wife's name. However, years of neglect had taken their toll on these things. The globe was cracked, the boxing glove was chipped, and the stone heart lay broken in two.

In the far corner Lorelli found a newer-looking

gravestone, black with white writing. She took a deep
breath and read the words.

Here Lie
Lord Mycroft Thornthwaite
Died 1996, aged 43
And his beloved wife,
Lady Martha Thornthwaite
Died 1996, aged 35
May both their souls rest easy

Lorelli was surprised to see that a bunch of flowers
was lying in front of the grave. 'Who laid these?' she
asked.

'I did,' replied Miss Wilde.

Lorelli felt a surge of guilt and terrible sadness. 'I'm
sorry,' she said, dropping to her knees. Agonising grief
tore through her heart and tears ran down her face. It
was the first time she had cried for her parents. Mr
Crutcher had always taught her and Ovid that grief
should be quiet and respectful, not open and gushing.
It felt overwhelming and scary to allow emotion to
take control of her body. She didn't know how long
she knelt there, lost in the trauma of her self-pity,
before she heard Adam speak.

'There you are,' he said.

Lorelli wiped her face and stood up. 'Where's she
gone?'

'Who?'

'The woman with the flowers.'

'I didn't see anyone,' said Adam. 'Oh, I see you've found your parents' grave.' He knelt down to look at it and Lorelli noticed his expression darken. '1996, the same year my mum died,' he said.

BAGSHAW'S END

Lorelli and Adam left the graveyard through a nearby gate and found themselves in a small winding lane. They walked down it and came to a tiny thatched cottage, surrounded by a densely overgrown garden. Creeping vines and ivy covered the building, as though the wild garden was slowly devouring the cottage.

'Do you think someone lives there?' said Lorelli, stopping to look at it.

'If they do they need a gardener,' replied Adam.

Lorelli read the name etched into the wooden sign on the front gate. 'Bagshaw's End,' she read aloud. 'This was where Mrs Bagshaw and her husband lived before she moved to Thornthwaite Manor.' She lifted the latch and opened the gate.

'What are you doing?' asked Adam.

'I'm going to take a closer look.' She made her way along the path, stepping over roots and branches, being careful to avoid the tall stinging nettles.

'Isn't this trespassing?'

'The house is part of our estate. You can't trespass on your own property. Besides, look at this garden, no one's been here in years.'

'What's that noise?' said Adam, noticing a low hum from the back of the garden.

'It sounds like a generator,' replied Lorelli, trying the door. After what the priest had said, and then finding Hedley Bagshaw's grave, she felt an overwhelming urge to look inside. 'This one's locked. Let's try the back.'

Walking around the cottage, they tried to see inside but all the windows were brown with dirt.

'I still don't feel right about this,' said Adam.

'Stay out here, then,' said Lorelli. Adam was starting to get on her nerves. She tried the back door and, to her surprise, found it was unlocked. She stepped into a small grubby kitchen and had a vision of what it would have looked like when Mrs Bagshaw lived there, with flowers on the windowsill, pots and pans so clean you could see your reflection in them, and enticing smells wafting from the oven. It was a stark contrast to the grimy, disused kitchen she was in now.

Adam followed her in. He ran a finger across a filthy counter. 'Disgusting, isn't it?'

Lorelli walked into the hallway and then into the front room, where the foliage had found its way inside through gaps in the window frame and spread its long green tentacles along the walls.

'This place must have been deserted for years,' said Adam.

Lorelli wiped a window to let more light in and saw, in the corner of the room, a pile of newspapers. She picked one up and read the front page. It was an old copy of the Hexford Express, filled with stories of minor incidents and local concerns. Her eyes were drawn to an article at the bottom of the front page.

'Listen to this,' she said, reading it out. 'Not to be missed in next week's paper, local historian Hedley Bagshaw delves into another fascinating family tree, uncovering details of how we used to live through personal stories of local families. In the next instalment of this popular series, Mr Bagshaw will be unravelling the history of local nobility, the Thornthwaite family.'

The paper was dated October 1996.

'That was the same year he died,' said Lorelli, remembering the date on the gravestone. She picked up the following week's paper and searched for the article. 'It's not in here.'

'Check all the pages. Maybe they moved where it was in the paper,' suggested Adam.

Lorelli systematically turned every page of the old, yellowed newspaper.

'There it is. That's his name, at the bottom of that page,' said Adam.

'This isn't the article,' said Lorelli. 'It's the obituaries.'

They read.

Hedley Bagshaw, local historian and printer of this newspaper, died tragically yesterday when he fell into the printing press while producing this edition of the newspaper. A highly valued member of the team and regular contributor to the paper, he leaves behind him a wife and a recently adopted baby girl, Hazel. Our thoughts are with them at this sad time.

Next to the article was a picture of a smiling man with kind eyes. Lorelli thought again about Father Whelan's accusation that Hedley had been killed by her father. Adam, who had been reading over Lorelli's shoulder, said, 'I'm going back to the manor.'

'Why?'

'This is all wrong, creeping around someone else's house. I should never have followed you in.'

'I'll come with you.'

'No,' said Adam firmly. 'I'd rather go alone. Here, use this to pay for your bus.' He threw her a pound coin and stormed out of the room.

Lorelli sat down. She turned the coin over in her hand, feeling confused by Adam's sudden change of tone and hurt by his decision to leave without her. He had brought her to the village and abandoned her there.

On the dusty coffee table in front of her was a pile of paper. She picked up the top piece. Realising what it was, she grabbed the whole pile and looked through, unable to believe what she was seeing. Each had a line-drawn design on it. One was of a tree, with a line running from a branch down to a small circle labelled in capital letters, *TRIGGER*. It was a design for the attack at the old oak tree. Another had a picture of a horse, with an arrow pointing to the underside of the saddle, with the word *POLLEN* beneath.

'Ovid,' said Lorelli to herself. She had often wondered where Ovid kept his designs. Now she knew.

THE HAMMER AND THE HIVE

Lorelli looked through the pages of diagrams and plans. She was in no doubt that they were Ovid's. Some of them she recognised. Some she didn't. They didn't all make sense to her, like the bike tube filled with honey, but they all had the hallmark of her brother's technically brilliant and murderous mind. She looked at one showing a hammer attached to a pole, next to a wooden box. Her eyes were drawn to the words next to it.

KILLER BEES' HIVE

Reading these words, Lorelli became aware that she could still hear the low hum coming from the back garden. She had dismissed the noise as some kind of generator. She had stopped listening, but tuning in again she realised what it was. It was the buzzing of bees.

Lorelli followed the sound out of the house, into the overgrown garden. She rounded a hedge and came to a sudden halt when she saw what was behind it. In front of her was a large rectangular box, alive with noise and activity as a constant stream of bees flew in and out of holes in the side.

Just like in the line drawing, the hive was balanced on top of a stool, which was carefully placed on a metal grate. Next to this was a vertical metal pole, with a spring running up it. Another pole was attached horizontally at the top, at the end of which was a hammer.

Lorelli gazed at it, wondering about its purpose. She took a step forward to get a closer look. Then another. Then one more.

She was getting uncomfortably close now but before she could turn back she felt the ground beneath her feet give way. She screamed as she slipped down into a hole and threw her arms out, but she couldn't get a grip. The hole wasn't very deep but it sloped at an angle. She felt her feet slip and she slid on her back, further underground. It all happened so quickly that before she knew what was going on, she was lying flat, looking up through a grate, directly underneath the hive.

The buzzing was even louder here and the sky was obscured by thousands of bees. She could hear a ticking noise and saw that the horizontal bar with the hammer on the end was moving back.

Tick-tick-tick, it went.

As it moved, it tightened the spring.

Tick-tick-tick.

Too late, Lorelli understood the design. Her fall had triggered the movement of the hammer. Once the maximum pressure had been reached the hammer would spring back and fly into the side of the beehive, knocking it off its stool and smashing it on to the grate, sending thousands of angry bees out. Scared and confused, the swarm would be ready to sting the first thing they came across. The whole thing was an elaborate trap designed to catch anyone who got too close to the beehive.

Tick-tick-tick.

Lorelli tried to climb out of the hole but her feet were wedged in. She clawed at the dirt with her fingernails but still couldn't move. Ovid had designed the trap well.

Tick-tick-tick.

She tried pushing the grate but realised that moving it would tip the stool and knock the hive on top of her. 'Help!' she shouted. 'I'm stuck. Help.'

No reply came.

She was alone.

The spring looked like it couldn't take much more. It was vibrating with the pressure. The hammer was about to swing.

Tick-tick . . . CLICK.

The spring reached its point of full tension and the hammer swung towards the hive.

With the knowledge that a hive of killer bees was about to descend on her, Lorelli could have been forgiven for crying, but her green eyes watched unflinchingly as the hammer crashed into the side of the hive, sending an army of bees gushing out like troops called to battle.

This is it, she thought, *this is how I die.*

Honey dripped down from the broken hive, landing on her upper lip, sticky, sweet and spicy. She wondered if it would be the last thing she tasted before she was stung to death.

A MOVEMENT IN THE WINDOW

Lying in the trap, awaiting her painful death, Lorelli suddenly felt two strong hands grab her shoulders and haul her out of the hole. She opened her eyes and saw the hive crash into the grate, sending a mushroom cloud of bees into the air. Gloved hands carried her away. Her saviour's face was obscured by a beekeeper's hood.

They reached the front of the cottage and Lorelli saw a tractor parked there. Her rescuer pulled off his hood.

'Have you been stung, Miss Lorelli?' said Tom Paine.

'Tom,' said Lorelli.

'Hello Miss Lorelli. Have you been stung?' he repeated.

'I don't think so.'

'Good, because you'd know about it if you had been. Now, you stay here and I'll go and sort out them bees.'

With which he lifted Lorelli up on to the tractor seat and headed back around the side of the house.

'Were they killer bees?' asked Lorelli, when he returned.

'Oh aye. Nasty little blighters too. I've been trying to track them down since we last saw them.'

'How do you track a bee?'

'Same as tracking any animal, with lots of patience and attention to detail.'

'What did you do to them?'

'I killed them.'

'Killed them?'

'Yes. You see they're illegal in this country and they don't get on with our domestic bees. So I sprayed them with insecticide and put them all to sleep. Shame in a way. I had to spray all the honey too. I'd love to know what it tastes like. What were you doing here anyway?'

'I saw the name on the gate,' said Lorelli. 'And after what the priest said . . .'

'Father Whelan?' interrupted Tom. 'Let me guess, he told you that your father had something to do with Hedley Bagshaw's death?'

'Yes,' said Lorelli, surprised that Tom already knew this.

'Well, you don't want to be taking heed of anything that old drunkard in a dress says. At the time he would tell anyone that would listen that he saw Lord Mycroft coming out of the printer's on the night Hedley died, but there's no truth in it. Firstly, that church is a good distance from the printer's and at the time the trees would have been covered in leaves. You try looking to see how clearly you can see across the road. Secondly, old Whelan always had it in for your father on account of having to pay rent for the vicarage. Thirdly, your mum and dad were in Venice at the time on honeymoon, so there's no way he had anything to do with it. That old priest is just a drunken troublemaker.'

Lorelli felt a huge sense of relief. Tom had always been a voice she could trust. It was comforting to hear him dismiss Father Whelan's accusations so offhandedly.

Tom's tractor was slow-moving and, on the way back to Thornthwaite Manor, several cars got stuck behind it, impatiently trying to overtake on the narrow lane. Eventually, Tom turned off the road up the dappled drive, towards Thornthwaite Manor allowing the cars to accelerate away. The sun was lower in the sky now, creating an orange glow.

When she got home, Lorelli looked for Adam, but was informed by Mr Crutcher that he had not yet returned.

'Mr Farthing has asked me to pass on his apologies that neither he nor his son will be joining you and your brother for dinner tonight,' Mr Crutcher added.

Lorelli was already sitting down at the dining-room

table when Ovid limped in with a crutch under one arm.

'Eventful day?' she said.

'Bearable,' replied Ovid, looking at his sister for a reaction.

'Adam and I went to Little Fledgling,' said Lorelli.

'I heard. Where is Adam?'

'I don't know,' admitted Lorelli. 'He came home alone.'

'Tired of you, did he?' said Ovid.

The twins consumed the rest of their dinner in an atmosphere of quiet mistrust. Afterwards Ovid suggested that they continue their chess game but Lorelli said she was tired and went to her bedroom.

ACCUSATIONS AND DENIALS

In the days that followed Lorelli's trip to the village, Ovid sensed that his sister had become even more wary of him. Adam was acting differently too and there was a discernable coldness between him and Lorelli.

Meanwhile, Ovid's number-one goal was to get into Lorelli's bedroom to see the proof that his sister was behind the bear attack.

Eventually, with his ankle healing, and his sister out enjoying her daily swim, Ovid was able to make it to the top of the central spire to his sister's bedroom door.

He crossed the room and opened her bureau, where he found the document that Mr Farthing had referred to. It was a request to purchase a bear from a zoo that was closing down. There were various letters about this and Ovid was still reading through the correspondence when the door opened and Lorelli entered.

'Get out,' she said, catching her breath.

Ovid looked up. 'My dearest sister,' he said, 'I'm disappointed in you. I thought we had a truce.'

'So did I,' countered Lorelli.

'So what's this?' Ovid held up the bundle of letters.

'I don't know. What is that?'

'It's a document showing that you purchased a bear from a zoo, Lorelli.'

'We both had plans before the truce but I cancelled all mine on our birthday.'

'Really?' said Ovid disbelievingly.

'I never went through with it,' said Lorelli.

'So the large brown bear roaming about in the woods is a coincidence, is it? Probably just here on holiday.'

'I don't know anything about that.'

'A likely story. I suppose you don't know anything about how my bike came to be filled with honey either?' snapped Ovid.

'Filled with honey?' said Lorelli, remembering the design she had found in Bagshaw's End. She knew better than to trust her brother but she began to feel that something else was going on here. 'They weren't your plans in Bagshaw's End, were they?'

'Bagshaw's what?'

'It's where Mrs Bagshaw used to live before she moved here. I thought you'd been using it to plan your attacks.'

'I've never been there.'

'There were plans for the booby-trapped tree, the killer bees and . . . a bike filled with honey.'

The twins stared at each other, their green eyes locked in concentration, both coming to the same conclusion.

'Since the truce, someone else has been trying to kill us,' said Lorelli, saying what they were both thinking.

Suddenly an explosion shook the building to its foundations, causing an oil painting on Lorelli's wall to crash to the floor. The twins maintained their stare, each trying to read the other's expression.

'What was that?' said Ovid.

'You tell me,' said Lorelli.

'Nurse Griddle, come quickly,' shouted Hazel's voice from downstairs.

Lorelli bolted out of the room, down the spiral stairs and the main staircase to where Hazel was standing in the hallway, looking distraught. Ovid limped after her. White smoke was billowing out of the drawing-room door. Mr Farthing appeared from the dining room. 'What is it?' he was saying. 'What's happened?'

'It's Adam,' replied Hazel tearfully.

'What? What about my boy?' demanded Mr Farthing, growing agitated.

'He was only playing it,' she said. 'I was at the door

listening, watching through the gap. I like the tunes he plays.'

'What are you babbling about? Speak, girl.' He grabbed her shoulders angrily.

'The piano . . . It just . . . It exploded,' she sobbed.

'Get out of the way.' Mr Farthing pushed her aside. Ovid and Lorelli followed him into the smoke-filled room. Ovid opened a window and the smoke dissipated enough to see that the front half of the piano was missing. Bits of it lay all over the room. Black and white keys lay scattered across the floor. And lying in the middle of the mess, his face blackened from the explosion, was Adam.

Mr Farthing fell to his knees and took his son in his arms. 'Adam? Adam?' he said desperately. 'Are you all right? Speak to me. Please.' He looked up at Lorelli and Ovid with fury in his eyes. 'You murderous children. You are just like your parents,' he snarled. 'Look what your terrible games have done to my boy.'

AN INSPECTOR CALLS

In spite of Nurse Griddle's attempts to treat Adam Farthing's injuries his father had not let her near him.

'But Mr Farthing, I will be able to help the child,' Nurse Griddle protested.

'I will not put my son's life in the hands of any of you people,' said Mr Farthing, shaking with anger and fear. Instead he used his mobile phone to call an ambulance.

When the ambulance arrived, two men carried Adam on a stretcher and drove away with him and Mr Farthing in the back. The twins stood outside the main door and watched it drive down the long gravel driveway.

'Do you thinking he played a wrong note?' said Ovid, with a wry smile.

'Tell me, honestly. Was it you? Did you booby-trap the piano?' said Lorelli.

'My darling sister . . .'

'Don't start that. Tell me truthfully. You knew that Adam liked to play it. You never liked him. Was it you?'

'No. What about you? This wasn't another one of your attacks on me gone wrong, was it?'

'I swear on our parents' grave that I had nothing to do with it.'

The twins' attention was drawn by the sound of a motor engine. An old-fashioned car was approaching up the driveway, moving slowly to avoid any loose stones bouncing up and damaging the immaculate paintwork.

'Thornthwaite Manor seems to have become remarkably busy this Easter,' said Ovid.

When the car stopped, a tall man in a brown suit stepped out. A thick moustache on his lip compensated for the lack of hair on his head.

'Good afternoon,' he said, closing the car door behind him. 'My name is Skinner . . . Detective Inspector Skinner. And I guess you are . . .' He flicked open a pad and glanced at it. 'Of course, you're Ovid and Lorelli. My my, how you've grown.'

'You're the policeman who saw our mother die,' said Lorelli, recognising the name at once.

'I'm sorry to say that is true. A beautiful woman, your mother. Very sad . . . tragic in fact.' Skinner bowed his head.

'Can we help you?' said Ovid curtly.

Again, Skinner consulted his notepad. 'I believe there was some kind of explosion that resulted in the hospitalisation of Adam Farthing.'

'Who told you that?' said Ovid.

'We had a call from a Mr Bernard Farthing. I'll have to interview everyone here.' He looked up at the manor. 'It's been a long time since my last visit.'

'It has indeed, Inspector,' said Mr Crutcher, appearing at the doorway. 'I'd have thought you'd have retired by now.'

'Mr Crutcher. I remember you of course,' said Skinner. 'May I see the crime scene?'

'Please come in.' Mr Crutcher beckoned Skinner up the steps and led him through the hall into the drawing room, where Hazel was on her knees picking up bits of piano.

'You, girl, get away from that,' barked Skinner. 'Don't touch a thing.'

'I was only tidying up,' she replied.

'Well, don't. This is a crime scene. Nothing should be touched.'

The twins followed Skinner into the room and Lorelli noticed that in spite of the chaos caused by the explosion, the game of chess on the far side of the room was undisturbed.

'I'm afraid, Detective Inspector Skinner, that you have got the wrong end of the stick,' said Mr

Crutcher. 'There's a perfectly logical explanation for this terrible accident.'

'I'm intrigued to hear how this could possibly be described as an accident,' said Skinner.

'Then allow me to explain. The piano is an antique. It was purchased by Lord Allegro Thornthwaite in the eighteenth century. A piano was still a relatively new instrument at the time, something of a fashionable accessory. This one was made by London instrumenters, Fob and Swine.' Mr Crutcher pointed to where the name had been written on the front of the piano but now lay smashed on the floor.

Lorelli and Ovid looked at each other. Neither had heard the piano's history before.

'A fascinating musical history,' said Skinner, 'but what relevance is all this? Unless Messrs Fob and Swine were in the habit of placing bombs in their pianos.'

'Piano-making was in its infancy. It was a time of experimentation. Each piano-maker had his own quirks. Some made square pianos, some four octaves, some five or six. There was much debate on the merits of pedals. Fob and Swine had an especially eccentric idea that the sound of the instrument could be made more dramatic by making a hollow chamber in the piano lid then filling it with a mixture of sulphur, charcoal and potassium nitrate.'

'That's gunpowder,' said Skinner.

'Correct.'

'You're telling me some pianos are filled with gunpowder?' said Skinner incredulously.

'This was the only one. You see, after producing this one for Lord Thornthwaite, Fob and Swine went bankrupt following an explosion in their warehouse.'

'All right,' said Skinner, 'so if this is true, why would it explode now?'

'Unlike young Master Thornthwaite, Adam Farthing has a rather enthusiastic style of playing. I did plead with him to abide by our rules, to stick with sombre, respectful pieces, but he is a hot-headed boy. I imagine the vigorous hammer action inside caused a spark and ... BANG ... the whole thing went up. As I say, a terrible accident.'

'I'll have to check this out and interview all of the staff,' said Skinner, who had been scribbling in his notepad. 'Excuse me, that's my phone.' Orchestral music was coming from his pocket. He put his pad away and retrieved a mobile phone from his pocket. 'Yes? Yes, I see ... At what time? Yes ... Right ... Of course ... Yes, I'm here now. I'll be there shortly.'

He hit the disconnect button and turned his gaze on the twins, before looking at Mr Crutcher. 'I'm afraid this has just got more serious. This is no longer simply a criminal enquiry.'

'What do you mean?' asked Lorelli.

'It is now a murder enquiry.'

'Murder?' said the twins, speaking as one.

'Yes, Adam Farthing is dead. Now, please vacate the room. It will be sealed off until further notice.'

ACT THREE

THE ALL-SKY JIGSAW

Shortly after Detective Inspector Skinner had delivered the shocking news of Adam Farthing's death, he ushered Lorelli and Ovid out of the drawing room and sealed it off with police tape.

Unsure what to do with herself, Lorelli went to the library and picked up her copy of *The Seven Dances of Franciska Tóth*, but when she sat down to read she found it difficult to concentrate on the words. There was too much to think about, so she sat there turning the pages, unable to take any of it in. Adam was dead. He was the only friend Lorelli had ever made. It didn't seem real. The grief she had grown up with felt damp and musty compared with this new wave of sadness that saturated her heart.

Ovid entered the room, carrying a brown briefcase in one hand and a cardboard box with a blue lid in the other. Lorelli slipped her book under a cushion and Ovid sat down in front of her. He put the briefcase down by his side, took the lid off the box and poured out its contents on to the table between them. Hundreds of jigsaw pieces spilled out.

'What are you doing?' asked Lorelli, coldly.

'I thought that since we were separated from our game of chess we could try this,' replied Ovid, turning the pieces face up.

Every single one was light blue.

'What is this?'

'It's a thousand-piece all-sky jigsaw,' replied Ovid, continuing to turn over the pieces.

When all the jigsaw pieces were face up, the twins found a corner each and searched for the connecting pieces. They sat in silence for some time until Lorelli spoke.

'We need to be able to trust each other,' she said.

'I was thinking exactly the same thing.' Ovid reached into his case and pulled out a wad of paper tied together with string.

'What's that?'

'Every plan I've ever made to kill you, every scheme I've devised, every design I've drawn.'

Lorelli took the pile of paper and rested it on her knee. She understood the significance of the gesture. She looked through the hand-drawn designs of countless ingenious methods to ensure her demise: traps to ensnare her; explosives to blow her up; chemical concoctions to poison her.

'I remember this one,' she said. 'The trap door in the dining room with the conveniently placed spike underneath.'

'That took me ages to get right,' said Ovid with a wry smile. 'And you still survived it.'

'And this was the time you put that deadly spider in the bathroom.'

'What happened to that?'

'Cowell ate it.'

Ovid laughed. 'So much for being deadly.'

The twins shared a smile, then Ovid said, 'What about you? I need to know I can trust you too.'

'I never kept my plans,' replied Lorelli.

'Then tell me something you've never told me before.'

Lorelli reached behind her and pulled out the copy of *The Seven Dances of Franciska Tóth* from behind the cushion. 'This is my favourite book. I've read it more times than I can remember. I've always kept it secret from you.'

Ovid stared at the book then reached into his briefcase a second time. He pulled out another copy of it, identical except for its plastic covering.

'Where did you get that?' asked Lorelli, stunned.

'Mother's bedside table. It's the book she was reading when she died.'

Lorelli took it and opened it. On the inside jacket was a piece of paper with the words Little Fledgling

Library printed on it, beneath which a number of dates had been stamped. The most recent was 19th April, 1996.

'That was the day our father died,' said Lorelli.

'What does it mean?' asked Ovid.

'I don't know. Perhaps nothing.' Lorelli shrugged. She looked down at the mess of blue jigsaw pieces. 'Our whole lives are like this jigsaw,' she said, 'fragments that fit together somehow.'

Ovid reached into his briefcase again and pulled out a yellowed piece of paper in a clear plastic folder.

'Father's will,' said Lorelli.

'I took it from Mr Farthing's things.'

He passed it to her and Lorelli read the typed words with their father's signature at the bottom.

'In the event of my death,' Lorelli read aloud. 'I, Lord Mycroft Thornthwaite, leave my entire fortune and estate to my wife, Lady Martha Thornthwaite. In the event of her death it shall be split equally between our children, Ovid and Lorelli Thornthwaite, upon their sixteenth birthday. Prior to that, the estate and management thereof will be entrusted to the guardianship of Mr Alfred Crutcher.' She looked up. 'But we know all this.'

'Read the paragraph below,' said Ovid.

Lorelli continued. 'If either twin should outlive the other the whole of the estate will pass to the surviving one. In the event of both of their deaths the estate will be divided equally between our loyal servants, Mr Alfred Crutcher, Mrs Hilda Bagshaw, Miss Eileen Griddle and Mr Thomas Paine.'

As she read the names, Lorelli's hands trembled. 'So they all get the inheritance if we die.'

'We can't trust anyone,' said Ovid. 'I bet Farthing's in on it too. That's why he didn't show us the will.'

'But the servants?' said Lorelli, in disbelief. 'If Mrs Bagshaw had wanted us dead she could have poisoned us years ago. Tom has always been there for us. Alfred has looked after us since we were children and Nurse Griddle has spent her life making us better.'

Ovid looked deep into his sister's eyes. 'Lorelli, we have spent our entire lives trying to murder each other and our servants have stood by and never spoken a word to discourage us.'

Lorelli looked down and shut her eyes for a moment. The mention of murder brought Adam's death back to her mind. 'I can't believe he's dead.'

Ovid put the will back in his case then reached a hand across the table and placed it on top of his sister's.

'I spent so much time devising methods of murder that I had forgotten what it meant for someone to die,' she said.

They remained still, with Ovid's hand gently over his sister's until the door opened and Inspector Skinner entered the room, closely followed by Mr Crutcher.

SKINNER'S INVESTIGATION

'Actually, Alfred, I would rather speak to the children alone,' said Skinner.

'As they are minors and I am their guardian, I will remain for the interview,' said Mr Crutcher, retreating to the corner of the room.

Skinner looked down at the puzzle between the twins. 'I used to love a good jigsaw when I was young. Nothing like it for a rainy day, is there?'

'You've sealed off our chess game,' said Ovid.

'All strictly necessary, I assure you. Now, I have to ask you both a few questions,' said Skinner, pulling out a notepad.

'Like an interrogation?' said Ovid eagerly.

Skinner smiled. 'I'm collecting witness statements from everyone. It's normal procedure.' He flipped open his notepad. 'Now, where were you when you heard this explosion?'

'We were both in my room,' said Lorelli.

'And what did you do after hearing it?'

'We came downstairs. Hazel and Mr Farthing were already there,' said Ovid.

'When was the last time you saw Adam alive?'

'At breakfast,' said Lorelli.

Skinner turned back to Ovid. 'You play the piano too, I understand?'

'Yes.'

'But it's never exploded before?'

'Obviously not,' replied Ovid.

'Did you know about the presence of gunpowder in its construction?' Skinner scribbled away in his pad.

'No, but it wouldn't surprise me. There are many hidden dangers in Thornthwaite Manor.' Ovid glanced over to where Mr Crutcher was standing quietly in the corner.

'Could anyone have tampered with the piano?'

'I suppose so.'

'What about your cook? Did she have a grudge against the Farthings?'

'Mrs Bagshaw?' said Lorelli. 'What has she to do with anything?'

'I understand that some nuts found their way into Adam Farthing's food recently, even though his father told Mrs Bagshaw that the boy was allergic.'

'That was an accident,' said Lorelli. 'Hazel didn't know.'

'Hazel,' said Skinner, flicking back through his notepad. 'Ah yes, Mrs Bagshaw's adopted daughter, the girl seen tampering with the evidence.'

'She was tidying up,' said Lorelli.

Skinner sat down at the table with the twins. He looked at the jigsaw pieces. 'If you don't mind my saying, you both seem surprisingly calm considering the circumstances.'

'Would you prefer it if we were crying and wailing?' said Lorelli.

'Not at all. I'm just used to more emotion from those who have witnessed a death.'

Mr Crutcher stepped forward and spoke. 'At Thornthwaite Manor, we wear our grief in a sombre, respectful manner, Inspector. Grief, for us, is very much a way of life.'

'I have a question for you, Inspector,' said Ovid.

'Of course,' said Skinner.

'If someone did booby-trap the piano, isn't that a rather obvious way to murder someone? I mean, whoever heard of an exploding piano?' said Ovid.

'Your question is based on two assumptions,' said Skinner. 'Firstly, that this was a murder attempt. Maybe it was practical joke, a childish prank gone wrong. Say it was, as you suggest, an intentional murder, your question implies that murderers are intelligent enough to avoid getting caught. In my experience there is nothing clever about murderers.

They do not spend time plotting brilliant plots and scheming brilliant schemes. In my experience, the one thing murderers have in common is stupidity. It is what gets them caught.'

A GOOD LUNCH

Standing on the steps in front of Thornthwaite Manor, watching Skinner's car drive away, Lorelli said, 'Do you think we should have spoken to him while we had the chance and told him about the other attacks?'

'No, we shouldn't say anything that the servants might overhear,' replied Ovid.

'Lunch will be served shortly, young master and mistress,' said a voice behind them.

They turned to see Mr Crutcher standing in the doorway.

Sitting down to the table they found that rather than the usual bland lunch of half-a-parsnip soup and yesterday's bread, the meal consisted of a delicious, well-seasoned minestrone soup, freshly baked bread, a generous amount of butter and sweet lemonade to wash it down.

'Wow. Did Mrs Bagshaw really cook this?' said Ovid.

'Mum was too upset to prepare lunch after the Inspector spoke to her,' said Hazel, ladling out the soup.

'Why was she upset?' asked Ovid.

'I don't know,' said Hazel. 'But he interviewed her longer than anyone else. When she came out, she was crying.'

'Crying? Why?' asked Lorelli.

'She said he had brought up lots of painful memories. She said he asked her about Mr Bagshaw.'

'Why would he care about her husband?' asked Ovid, tearing off a piece of bread and dunking it in his soup.

'I can't say, but she's never let me prepare lunch myself before.'

'It's delicious. Thank you.' Lorelli took a sip from her spoon.

'If you don't mind, I'd better see how Mrs Bagshaw is now,' said Hazel.

'Of course,' said Lorelli.

Hazel left the room.

'What's Skinner up to?' said Ovid.

'I don't know but I think we should go and see him.'

'Where?'

'I saw the police station when I was visiting the village. If he's not there, they'll know where to find him.'

'How can we get to the village without asking one of the servants?'

'We'll catch the bus,' said Lorelli.

A FREE BUS RIDE

Following Ovid down to the main road, being careful to avoid getting spotted, Lorelli felt a strong sense that life had changed. Trusting no one but her twin, it was as though the whole focus of her life had shifted. That which was sharp had become blurred. That which had been blurred was coming increasingly into focus.

When the bus appeared around the corner, Ovid asked, 'What happens now?'

'It's simple,' said Lorelli, remembering what Adam had said. 'You stick out your arm, pay your money and sit down.'

'What money?'

Lorelli's heart dropped and so did her arm. She had forgotten about money.

'Is there none inside that?' asked Lorelli, indicating the briefcase that Ovid was still carrying.

'No. The only thing in here is the will and Mother's copy of that book you like so much.'

The bus's airbrakes hissed as it pulled in alongside them. The doors opened automatically and the bearded driver said, 'I don't pick up many from this stop. I almost didn't see you.'

The twins looked up at the man.

'Hop on then,' he said cheerfully.

'We don't have any money,' said Lorelli.

'I see,' said the bus driver. 'Hold on a minute, you're not them Thornthwaite kids, are you?' He said it almost like it was an accusation. The twins fought the urge to turn and run.

'Yes,' replied Ovid. 'What of it?'

'I pay rent to you lot,' he said. 'I've wanted to buy my house off you for years now, but you've never let me.'

'Mr Crutcher looks after the estate until we're old enough,' said Ovid.

'How long's that, then?' asked the bus driver.

'We inherit when we turn sixteen,' said Ovid.

'How old are you now?'

'Thirteen,' Lorelli replied.

'I tell you what, then,' said the bus driver, smiling, 'you can have all the free bus journeys you like if you let me buy my house when you're old enough.'

'It's a deal,' said Lorelli.

The bus driver grinned and offered his hand. The twins got on the empty bus, shook the driver's hand and sat down at the back.

The bus took a long winding route to the village, stopping every so often and picking up more people. A family got on and a brother and sister sat down in front of them. They were playing with a handheld computer game. It intrigued Lorelli, who had never seen one before. She thought how much else she and Ovid had missed out on, growing up in such isolation from the outside world. At first the brother and sister laughed about the game, then the sister wanted to play with it and they squabbled until their mother had to take it off them. Lorelli wondered what she and Ovid would have been like if their parents had survived. Would they have had a normal childhood, laughing and fighting and being told off, rather than living a life of quiet, sinister plotting?

When they arrived in the central square of Little Fledgling, the bus driver shouted, 'Last stop,' and everyone got off. As they left he said, 'Don't forget our deal, now.'

The twins promised not to and stepped off the bus.

LITTLE FLEDGLING LIBRARY

Standing in the village square, Lorelli saw a sign for *Little Fledgling Library*. 'Can I have Mother's book?' she said.

'Why?' asked Ovid. He pulled the book out of the briefcase.

'I'm going to return it. It won't take a minute.'

'What's the point of that?'

'It's not ours and it's very overdue. Besides, doesn't it make you wonder why Mother took a book out of the library when she already owned a copy?'

'Maybe she didn't know there was a copy in our library.'

'Maybe.'

Ovid handed her the book. 'I'll wait here,' he said, sitting down on a bench.

'Don't be long.'

'Don't you want to come in?'

'Not really. I'm here to find Skinner, not return

library books.'

Lorelli left him outside, secretly pleased that he wasn't coming with her. She had not been entirely honest about her reasons for wanting to go to the library. All her life she had wondered whether Imelda Gaunt had written any other books. Suddenly, with Little Fledgling Library in sight, she needed to find out.

Stepping through the doors her initial feeling was one of disappointment. She had imagined a public library to be more impressive than the one at Thornthwaite Manor. She was expecting towers of shiny brand-new books instead of Thornthwaite's old leather-bound hardbacks. But the books looked in worse condition than those she was used to. And they all had dirty plastic covers, which made even the new ones look old.

'Hello again, my dear,' said Miss Wilde, from behind the counter, looking every bit as friendly and dishevelled as the last time she had seen her. 'I'm so glad you've come.'

'I came to return this book,' said Lorelli, handing over *The Seven Dances of Franciska Tóth*.

Miss Wilde took it. 'My my, I haven't seen this book for a while.'

'It's a little overdue.'

'Well, never mind.' Miss Wilde turned it over in her hands. 'It doesn't look like a very good book anyway.

I'll probably just throw it away rather than waste shelf space on it.'

'You can't,' said Lorelli.

Miss Wilde looked at the blurb on back. 'A story about a brave young Hungarian girl who wants more than anything to dance,' she read. 'It doesn't sound very interesting.'

'But it's a beautiful story.'

'Is it indeed? Well, in my experience these days people want to read about exciting things: detectives, pirates, wizards . . . not silly little girls who want to ballet dance.'

'Franciska's not silly,' said Lorelli. 'It's my favourite book in the world and I won't return it if you're just going to throw it away.' She snatched the book out of Miss Wilde's hands.

'Your favourite book in the world?' Miss Wilde's eyes widened with surprise.

'Yes, I love it . . . Except for the ending.'

'You wish it had a happier ending?'

'So you have read it?'

'My dear girl,' said Miss Wilde, tears forming in her eyes. 'I wrote it.'

IMELDA GAUNT

Ovid had grown tired of waiting outside the library. Lorelli should have only taken a minute. Thinking that she had probably got distracted, he decided to go and get her.

As he entered, Lorelli was standing at the counter talking to a woman dressed in messily mismatched clothes. The woman turned and looked at him. Lorelli turned too.

'Ovid,' she said, 'this is Imelda Gaunt. I mean, Miss Wilde. I mean . . . She wrote the book.' Ovid had never seen his sister so excited. 'She wrote *The Seven Dances of Franciska Tóth*.'

'Pleased to meet you,' said Ovid.

'And you, my dear,' said Miss Wilde.

'Lorelli, do I have to remind you why we've come to the village?' said Ovid.

'I know but this is . . . what is your real name?' she said, looking at Miss Wilde.

'Wilde is my real name. Imelda Gaunt is as much an invention as Franciska Tŏth.'

'Why did you write under a different name, then?' asked Lorelli.

'I was scared,' said Miss Wilde. 'If the world hated my story I wanted to be able to hide from it. As it turned out, my book wasn't so much hated as ignored. No one reviewed it, very few people sold it and even fewer bought it. The worst fate for a book is to go unread.'

'But it's a wonderful book. I came here to find out if Imelda Gaunt had ... if you had written anything else.'

'That's sweet of you but no, I didn't and I never plan to. Like Franciska, I tried and I failed.'

Lorelli remembered what Adam had said about the author being successful. 'But my friend said that the book had made you rich and that you were ...' She stopped herself saying how Adam had described her as tall and beautiful too. She didn't want to hurt Miss Wilde's feelings.

'Your friend?' asked Miss Wilde.

'Adam Farthing. His father is your accountant.'

Miss Wilde laughed. 'I'm afraid I have no need of an accountant and I've never met anyone of that name. Farthing, you say?'

'Come on,' said Ovid impatiently. 'We should be going.'

'There must be a fine for the library book,' said Lorelli.

Miss Wilde typed something into a computer and looked at the screen. She smiled. 'I think we'll have to waive the charge,' she said. 'It's rather high.'

'We can pay,' said Lorelli. 'Not now, but when we come into our inheritance.'

'It's not your fine to pay,' replied Miss Wilde.

'It's only fair that our mother's debt should pass to us,' said Lorelli. 'We want to pay. You can buy some new books with the money.'

'It's not your mother's to pay either,' said Miss Wilde.

'Then whose is it?' asked Ovid.

'According to this it was taken out ten years ago by a Mrs R Farthing. Isn't that the name of your friend?'

'Mrs Farthing? You think it could be Adam's mum?' Lorelli asked Ovid.

'I don't know but we should go and find Skinner.' Ovid pulled his sister's sleeve.

'It was nice to see you again, Miss Wilde,' said Lorelli.

'And you,' said Miss Wilde. 'I'm glad you like my book.'

Lorelli and Ovid began to leave, when Lorelli paused and turned. 'Why couldn't it end happily for Franciska?' she asked.

'You say you've read it a number of times. Have you

ever tried to imagine a happy ending?'

'Yes. I even tried to write one.'

'So did I,' said Miss Wilde. 'I tried and tried to give Franciska a happy ending but it never worked.'

'But you're the author,' protested Lorelli.

'Characters have a life of their own,' said Miss Wilde. 'You stop being in complete control of them the moment they appear on the page. From the first sentence Franciska was condemned to an unhappy ending. For some people, tragedy is prewritten. It's in their stars. Franciska was just one of those characters.'

CONVERSATION IN THE STATION

Lorelli had read a good few mysteries in her life, but in those books the question was: *whodunnit*? In the real-life mystery that was unfolding in front the twins, it seemed to Lorelli that the question was more like *who-dun-what*? Every clue they uncovered made it less clear what the mystery was that they were attempting to solve.

'What was Mrs Farthing's library book doing in our mother's bedroom?' said Lorelli, as they walked from the library to the police station.

'And what was Mother's bookmark doing inside her book?' countered Ovid.

'How do you know it was hers?'

Ovid showed her the piece of paper with the two bars of music. 'It was Mother's tune. Tom remembered her playing it.'

'I never knew she composed music.'

'There are lots of things we don't know about our

parents.'

'Mother must have known Mr Farthing's wife.'

'Well, Mr Farthing is the family lawyer. Perhaps she borrowed it from his wife,' suggested Ovid.

'But why borrow a book she already owned?'

'I don't know,' admitted Ovid.

The twins fell silent, lost in thought until they arrived at the village police station.

'It's a bit small, isn't it?' Ovid looked at the tiny building, no larger than a garden shed.

'Skinner's inside,' said Lorelli.

The Inspector was standing, talking to a uniformed policeman who sat behind a desk. Skinner was trying to lean over the desk, but the size of the police station and the position of a filing cabinet were preventing him from doing so.

Cautiously, the twins crept closer to the open window to hear what they were saying.

'Look, sir, you know the rules,' said the seated policeman.

'Come on, Sergeant, what harm will it do?' said Skinner.

'Oh all right,' the sergeant said with a sigh.

'That's very good of you,' said Skinner.

There was a shuffling as the two men rearranged themselves in the minuscule room so that the sergeant could get to the filing cabinet behind Skinner.

'Ah, here we are,' said the sergeant. 'Mrs Ruth

Farthing, wife of Bernard, mother of Adam. She jumped off Devil's Leap. Very sad, but nothing suspicious about it.'

'Oh yes, I do remember now. Is there anything to connect her with Hedley Bagshaw?' Skinner peeked over the top of the file.

'Hedley Bagshaw? That printer chap who died at work?'

'That's the one,' said Skinner.

'Hold on, I'll check the file.' There were some more sounds of shuffling paper and filing-cabinet doors opening and shutting. 'Ah, here we are . . . No, nothing I can see. It was an accident at work. Fell into the printing press. Nothing untoward . . . Unless you count this.' He held out a piece of paper.

'What is it?'

'A statement made by Father Whelan. Crazy old kook. We only made a note of it to keep the old fool happy.'

'What does it say?'

'He claimed to have seen Lord Thornthwaite and an unknown woman leaving the printer's on the night that Hedley died.'

'Did no one ever follow it up?'

'Of course, but the thing was, His Lordship was out of the country at the time on honeymoon with his wife. You'll remember her, of course?'

'Lady Thornthwaite?' said Skinner. 'Yes, she was my

first case here. I was there when she died. What about this unknown woman that Whelan mentioned?'

'As I say, we never chased it up, sir. Father Whelan is overly fond of the communion wine, if you ask me,' said the sergeant. 'Why the sudden interest in all this, anyway? It's not like you're a copper any more. You should be enjoying your retirement. That's what I'd be doing in your place.'

'Once a copper always a copper,' said Skinner, opening the door and leaving. 'Thank you, Sergeant.'

SKINNER'S RENDEZVOUS

Ovid and Lorelli followed Skinner down the road, keeping a safe distance to avoid being seen.

'So he's not an inspector any more,' whispered Lorelli.

'And yet he is still inspecting,' said Ovid.

Skinner turned right along the path that led up through the graveyard to the church. Lorelli and Ovid followed him, ducking behind the gravestones. Skinner knocked on the door but there was no answer, so he walked around the side to another door and knocked again. This time Father Whelan came to the door.

'Yes?' said the priest.

'Father Whelan, I'd like to ask you a few questions about Hedley Bagshaw. May I come in?' replied Skinner.

'Hedley Bagshaw? Certainly.' Father Whelan opened the door wide. 'Come in, come in.'

The door shut behind them. Lorelli and Ovid crept closer. They looked through a window, where they could see the two men talking, but with all the windows shut they couldn't hear what was being said, so they retreated to a gravestone and waited for Skinner to appear.

'What do you think he's up to?' said Lorelli.

'I don't know but he seems more interested in Mrs Bagshaw's husband than the exploding piano,' said Ovid.

The door opened and the twins heard light classical music. Skinner stepped out and pulled his phone from his inside pocket. 'Excuse me, Father, I'll be back in one moment.'

Skinner took several steps away from the doorway and answered the phone. 'Skinner Investigations,' he said quietly. 'Lionel Skinner speaking... Ah, hello, yes... I'm rather busy at the moment... I see, well, yes, I'm in the village... OK... If you insist, I'll meet you outside the church... Five minutes? Fine.' He ended the call.

'Sorry, Father,' he said, turning back to address the priest. 'Something's come up. I'll be back shortly.'

'I'll be right here working on Sunday's sermon, my son. It's about the dangers of greed,' said Father Whelan.

'Sound riveting,' said Skinner, walking to the road, where he found a bench and sat down.

'Skinner Investigations?' whispered Lorelli. 'He's a private detective.'

'Then he must be working for someone,' replied Ovid. 'But who?'

The twins were by now hiding behind a low wall, from where they could see the back of Skinner's bald head. Hearing a car approach, they ducked down. They heard it stop and cautiously looked up to see an old, rusty, dust-coloured car. Mr Farthing stuck his head out of the window, banging the top of it against the frame.

'Afternoon Bernard,' said Skinner.

'Hello Lionel,' replied Mr Farthing, leaning over and opening the door from the inside. 'Would you mind getting in? I'd like a word in private.'

Skinner sat in the passenger seat and slammed the door shut. Mr Farthing attempted to turn the car around, turning a simple three-point turn into a complex manoeuvre involving seven or eight turns and knocking over a roadside bin in the process, spilling its contents over the pavement. 'Bother,' he said, sticking his head out of the window to assess the damage.

'You're so useless,' said a voice from inside the car.

'Who was that?' whispered Ovid. 'I can't see anyone except those two.'

'It sounded like . . .' Lorelli began.

'Sorry about that,' said Mr Farthing, easing down

on the accelerator again, reversing further over the bin.

'There was a time when I would have booked you for criminal damage for that,' said Skinner jokingly.

'Honestly, you're such a clumsy oaf,' said the third voice.

'It's Adam,' whispered Lorelli, spotting the top of Adam Farthing's fair hair through the car window.

THE BAGSHAW CONNECTION

On the bus back to Thornthwaite Manor, the twins discussed what they had witnessed by the church.

'I think they planted the bomb in the piano themselves in order to fake Adam's death,' said Ovid. 'That's why Mr Farthing wouldn't let Nurse Griddle near him.'

'They were all acting... Mr Farthing, Inspector Skinner... Adam,' said Lorelli.

Ovid fought down the urge to gloat that he had been right all along about Adam. Looking at his sister, he understood that for a few days of her life Lorelli had enjoyed having a friend, someone she believed genuinely liked her without an ulterior motive.

'But what did they gain from pretending Adam was dead?' she asked.

'Well, it gave Skinner an excuse to question everyone.'

'But about what?' Lorelli clung to the seat in front

as the bus swung around a corner and drove over the bridge, out of the village.

'I don't know but it explains why he didn't ask much about the piano.'

'It was Mrs Bagshaw he wanted to speak to,' said Lorelli. 'He spoke to her for much longer than anyone else and she was upset because he had been asking her about her husband.'

'You think the Farthings blew up our antique piano just so Skinner could ask Mrs Bagshaw a few questions about her dead husband?'

'It does sound a little wasteful, but think about it, Mrs Bagshaw never leaves the manor. Alfred shops for her. Hazel signs for deliveries. It can't be easy to get near her.'

'But why would anyone want to ask her anything, anyway?' asked Ovid. 'She's only a cook.'

Walking from the bus stop to the manor the twins spotted Tom Paine, driving his red lawnmower.

'Stay out of sight.' Ovid ducked down and tugging at Lorelli's sleeve.

'But it's Tom.'

'We can't trust anyone.'

Lorelli found it particularly difficult to suspect Tom of plotting against them but she knew her brother was right. Life had changed. Until they found out what was going on they could no longer trust anyone, not even Tom, so they hid until he had passed out of sight.

When they stepped into the hallway, Mr Crutcher greeted them. 'I hope you have been making the most of this fine weather, young master and mistress. There is a storm approaching from the east.'

'Which room was Adam staying in, Alfred?' asked Lorelli, not wanting to spend any more time with any of the servants than was necessary.

'Master Farthing was in the yellow suite in the west wing.'

'Thank you,' said Ovid, following his sister down the corridor.

Inside the room, they set about searching for clues. Ovid looked inside drawers while Lorelli rifled through a suitcase that had been tucked away inside a cupboard.

'This is that school he was always talking about,' said Ovid, holding up a glossy brochure with a picture of a stately looking building on the front and the words, *Welcome to Saint Swivels, The Finest Schooling Establishment in England*, printed in fancy swirly writing. He opened it and read out loud.

Saint Swivels has excellent facilities, including four football fields, eight basketball courts and twenty tennis courts. It has a science lab, a gym, and an Olympic-sized swimming pool. It even has a working farm on site. Every Friday, students can enjoy riding lessons. Our staff are second to none, including a tennis coach, who used to rank eighteenth in the world and a world-class pianist as our principal music teacher.

'Do you know, I have a feeling that this leaflet is the closest Adam's ever got to that school,' said Lorelli, continuing to look through the suitcase. There was nothing in the main compartment, but searching the zipped pockets she found a plastic folder. She pulled it out. Ovid stopped what he was doing and watched as she unzipped it and poured out the various scraps of paper. Some were torn out of notepads, others were corners of magazine pages. Every piece of paper had a line drawing of the same man's face.

'Who is it?' asked Ovid. 'I don't recognise him.'

'It's Hedley Bagshaw. I saw his picture in the paper.'

'Mrs Bagshaw's husband? Why would Adam have drawings of him?'

'His mum did them. She was an artist. That must have been why Adam suddenly left Bagshaw's End after he saw the picture. That's why Skinner was asking Mrs Bagshaw so many questions.'

'What do you mean?'

'They think Hedley Bagshaw killed Mrs Farthing,' said Lorelli.

'Why would he do that?' said Ovid.

'I don't know but it's time we spoke to Mrs Bagshaw ourselves, don't you think?' said Lorelli.

THE KITCHEN

In their entire lives, Lorelli and Ovid had only been into the kitchen at Thornthwaite Manor once. Several years ago, Ovid had ventured down after reading that it was possible to make a bomb out of baking powder. Following him and seeing what he was up to, Lorelli had gone in search of sharp knives to attach to the blades of a windmill she had constructed and placed outside the barn where Ovid had been building his bomb. As it transpired, the bomb had gone off early, when neither twin was in the vicinity, blowing up the windmill and sending its knives flying into the neighbouring trees.

Now, with Lorelli clutching one of Mrs Farthing's pencil drawings of Hedley Bagshaw, the twins entered the kitchen and found Mrs Bagshaw dicing an onion in preparation for dinner. The cook wiped away the tears that were streaming down her face with a grim-looking dishcloth.

'Hello my dears,' she said. 'These onions that Tom's grown are far too strong. Look at me. I'm crying like a baby. What brings you down here? Dinner won't be ready for at least an hour.'

'We'd like to know what Skinner was asking you about?' said Ovid directly.

'Oh, I don't want to go through all that again,' said Mrs Bagshaw. 'Horrible man.'

'We understand that it's upsetting for you,' said Lorelli, 'but it's important. What did he want?'

Mrs Bagshaw dabbed her eyes again with the dish-cloth. 'He asked me about poor, dear Hedley. I couldn't think what that had to do with anything but he seemed to have it in his head that Hedley knew Mr Farthing's wife. I can't think why. I don't think they ever met.'

'I think they did. This is one of her pictures,' said Lorelli, handing Mrs Bagshaw the sketch.

'My darling Hedley,' she said sadly. 'Why would Ruth have drawn this? He was never here when she used to come to the manor.'

'Mrs Farthing came here? Why?' said Lorelli.

'For the sitting, of course.'

'What sitting?' said Ovid.

'When she came to paint the portrait of your parents.'

Ovid and Lorelli looked at each other.

'She painted the portrait of our parents?' said Lorelli.

'That's right, I thought you knew,' said Mrs Bagshaw. 'She spent a several weeks here. She seemed like a nice enough lady. She was certainly very taken with the manor. And I thought she did a good job with the painting, quite a good likeness of both of them, but I don't know much about art.'

'She jumped off Devil's Leap,' said Lorelli.

'I know. Isn't it awful? Imagine taking your own life when you have a little child. Adam can't have been much more than a baby at the time.'

'And that's what Skinner was asking about?' said Ovid.

'Oh no, he kept asking silly questions about poor Hedley and whether he knew Mrs Farthing and where we both were on the night she died.'

'What did you say?' asked Lorelli.

'I told him the truth, that as far as I know they never did meet.'

'What about the night she died? Where was he?'

Fresh tears sprang to Mrs Bagshaw's eyes. 'He was in the churchyard.'

'The churchyard?' said Ovid.

'He was ... already dead,' she managed to say between sobs.

THE PORTRAIT

The Thornthwaite twins had gazed up at the painting of their parents every single day of their lives but as they entered the portrait room now, they looked at it differently. They didn't search their mother's face for some clue as to why she murdered their father. Nor did they look at their father and wonder what kind of man he had been. They didn't look at the picture at all. They looked at the paint, at the broad strokes that made up the background and the fine touches which went into the detail of the faces and clothes and wondered what they said about the artist.

'It's all death. This picture, this room, this manor,' said Lorelli. 'Everyone in these paintings is dead. Every artist that painted them is dead. We have grown up believing this room shows our family, but all it shows is death. We are thirteen years old, Ovid. Thirteen! We should be out playing with friends. We should be making up games, having fun, living our lives . . . not living in this morbid museum.'

'We can't help who we are,' said Ovid quietly.

'No, but we can choose who we want to be.'

Ovid remembered how he had walked in on Mr Farthing crying while looking at the picture. 'Mr Farthing knew that his wife painted this picture,' he said.

'Of course I did,' said Mr Farthing, entering the room. 'And how I wish I could go back and stop her.'

The twins turned to face him.

'I remember when she first came to Thornthwaite Manor,' continued the oversized lawyer. 'That night at home she was so excited by it all. She had never seen such opulence.' He shook his head sadly. 'I wish she had never set foot inside this terrible place.'

'Why did you hire Skinner?' asked Ovid.

'I didn't come here to answer your questions,' replied Mr Farthing. 'I came back to collect Adam's things.'

'Poor Adam. You must be awfully upset.' Lorelli watched him carefully for a reaction.

'Well, yes . . .' said Mr Farthing, awkwardly. 'In fact, because of his death I will be resigning as your lawyer.'

'Why did you hire a detective?' Ovid perisisted.

'I don't know what you're talking about.' Mr Farthing turned to leave.

'We know the truth,' said Lorelli. 'We know that Adam isn't dead.'

Mr Farthing stopped in the doorway and turned to face them. 'He tells such terrible lies,' he muttered.

'What other lies?' said Lorelli.

'Adam has a . . .' Mr Farthing faltered for a moment. 'A . . . a colourful imagination. He gets it from his mother, I believe.'

'There are other qualities I get from my mother,' said Adam Farthing, striding into the room. 'Like a desire to better myself. It's a quality which you sadly lack, Father.'

ADAM FARTHING'S AMBITION

There was no outward change to Adam's appearance from the last time Lorelli had seen him. His hair was as blond and wavy as before, his eyes as blue, his chin as square. And yet, with all she now knew of him it might have been a different person that strode into the portrait room.

'Hello Adam,' said Lorelli, coldly.

'Back from the dead, I see,' said Ovid.

'Now, son, I thought we agreed that you would stay out of sight,' said Mr Farthing.

'As usual father, you're ruining everything,' said Adam.

'I'm acting in your best interests,' replied Mr Farthing.

'Well, don't. I don't need your help and I don't need you.'

Mr Farthing looked as if something had become lodged in his throat and was causing tears to spring to his eyes. 'Your words can be very hurtful,' he said, blinking back the tears.

'Why did you pretend to be dead?' asked Lorelli.

Adam turned to look at her. 'Lorelli, I'm so sorry. I never meant to upset you.'

'Well, you didn't,' lied Lorelli. 'What do you want?'

'I want to explain. I really like you, Lorelli.'

'You mean you really like my inheritance.'

'Son, it's time to leave,' said Mr Farthing.

'No!' shouted Adam. 'I'm tired of you messing everything up.'

'Adam Farthing, I am your father. You will show me some respect,' barked Mr Farthing.

'You don't deserve respect,' spat Adam. 'A real father would have supported me. A real father would have sent me to a decent school. A real father would care who killed his wife.' He shouted these last words in his father's face.

Mr Farthing shook his head. 'There are things you don't understand about your mother.'

'I understand enough. I know that you never provided for her.'

'It wasn't in her nature to be satisfied.'

'You mean she wouldn't settle for second best,' said Adam.

'You think that the wealth that surrounds you here would make you happy, do you? Well, look at these two. Do they look happy?' Mr Farthing pointed a trembling finger at Lorelli and Ovid.

'I would be happy if I had what they had,' said Adam.

Mr Farthing shook his head sadly. 'That's why I didn't want to bring you here. I remember the effect it had on your mother. She couldn't talk about anything else afterwards. Your mother couldn't put it out of her head. She was driven mad by jealousy. It was the same year that she took her own life.'

'It's not true. She didn't kill herself. Mum was murdered.'

'No, she wasn't,' said Mr Farthing calmly, sounding like a man who had had this argument many times before.

'Skinner would have found out who did it if you hadn't interfered,' said Adam.

'Skinner only cares about getting paid,' said Mr Farthing. 'You had no right to hire him in the first place.'

'Adam hired him? Not you?' said Lorelli.

'Yes,' said Adam. 'All my life I've been searching for the man in my mother's sketches. Then, in Bagshaw's End with you, I saw a photo of Hedley Bagshaw. I recognised him immediately.'

'So, why did you blow up my piano?' said Ovid incredulously.

'I didn't. Mr Crutcher was right about the piano being dangerous,' said Adam. 'It blew up because of the way I was playing it, just as he said. But then I realised that by acting injured it would give Skinner a chance to interrogate the servants. Otherwise Mr Crutcher would never have let him in. Nothing is more important to me than finding out who killed my mother.'

'Remember what the counsellor told you,' said Mr Farthing. 'It's understandable that you want to blame someone else for your mother's death. But no one else is to blame. Not me, not you and certainly not poor Mrs Bagshaw's husband. Your mother took her own life because she was unhappy, but it's not your fault.'

There was a moment's pause when these words seemed to linger in the air before Skinner stepped through the doorway and said, 'Actually, Bernard, I think I may have discovered your wife's killer.'

'You,' snarled Mr Farthing. 'You won't get a single penny from us. You should never have taken a case from a child.'

'I'm fifteen,' protested Adam.

'You'll pay me once I reveal what I have discovered, if only to keep me quiet,' said Skinner. 'You may come in now, Father.'

SKINNER'S DISCOVERY

'Murderers and thieves, all of them,' said Father Whelan, moving like a crow with an injured wing as he entered the room in his black robe. 'The history of the Thornthwaites is one of murder and skulduggery.' He pointed up at one of the portraits on the far side of the room. 'Lord Royston Thornthwaite, born 1872, died 1934,' he said dramatically, 'hanged his own father in order to get his inheritance.' The priest moved to another portrait. 'Lord Silas Thornthwaite, born 1912, died 1972, a man so mean spirited that he once shut down the local orphanage in the dead of winter because they couldn't afford the rent.' He moved to the picture of the twins' parents. 'Lord Mycroft Thornthwaite,' he said in a hissing whisper, 'killed Hedley Bagshaw in 1996 only to be murdered by his own wife later that year.'

'Get out of our home,' said Lorelli.

'Renounce your family's ways,' said Father Whelan,

waving his arms in the air dramatically.

'Why have you brought this crazy priest here?' said Adam to Skinner.

'Because Father Whelan holds a vital clue regarding this case,' Skinner replied.

'This is ridiculous,' said Mr Farthing. 'There is no case.'

'Ah, but there is,' said Skinner. 'Father Whelan saw two people leaving the printer's the night Hedley Bagshaw died. He recognised Lord Thornthwaite but not the woman he was with. Please, Adam, show him the picture of your mother.'

Adam pulled out his mother's pencil-drawn self-portrait and held it out for the wild-eyed priest to see.

Father Whelan leant forward, peered at it then recoiled in horror. 'That's her,' he said. 'That's the woman who was with Lord Thornthwaite that night.'

'What does this mean?' said Adam.

'Ruth Farthing was with Lord Thornthwaite the night Hedley Bagshaw died,' said Skinner. 'It stands to reason that she witnessed him do it.' He paused for dramatic effect. 'Possibly she helped him.'

'This is conjecture. You don't know any of it for sure,' said Mr Farthing.

'You're right,' said Skinner. 'We may never know who did what that night, but we do know that your wife and Lord Thornthwaite were there. We know that the following year your wife died, therefore I believe that Lord Thornthwaite, having murdered Hedley Bagshaw, killed Mrs Farthing to prevent her giving him away.'

'How dare you say such things?' said Mr Farthing angrily.

'I was hired to find out the identity of your wife's killer.'

'I thought I made it perfectly clear in the car that Adam should not have hired you,' said Mr Farthing. 'My boy is dreadfully disturbed by his mother's death. I have tried everything I can: psychiatrists, counsellors ... anyone who might help him come to terms with the fact that Ruth took her own life ...'

'You don't understand,' shouted Adam.

'I do. Your denial is understandable. No son wants to believe that his mother would rather die than be with him. It's hard for a husband too but we have to accept the truth. She killed herself.' Mr Farthing's voice quivered with every word.

'If you do not pay me for the work I have done I will go public with my discovery,' said Skinner.

'Pay you?' shouted Mr Farthing furiously. 'You expect to get paid for these flimsy accusations?'

'My bones grow old but my eyes are sharp. Your wife was with Lord Thornthwaite that evening,' said Father Whelan.

'Our father was abroad that night,' said Ovid.

'That's right. He was on his honeymoon,' added

Lorelli. 'So whoever you saw, it wasn't him. Besides, how come you were the only one to see him?'

'He wasn't,' said a voice behind them.

The twins, Father Whelan, Skinner, Mr Farthing and Adam turned around to see Nurse Griddle standing in the doorway, her face as unsmiling as ever.

'What do you mean?' asked Ovid.

'I was in the village that night,' she replied, stepping into the room. 'I saw Lord Thornthwaite go into the printer's.'

'Ah-ha. Then you can confirm that Mrs Farthing was with him too?' said Skinner.

'No.' Nurse Griddle shook her head. 'Lord Thornthwaite entered with Hedley Bagshaw himself.'

'But if you saw him, why didn't you report it to the police?' asked Lorelli.

'Because I left the village that day. I didn't hear about Hedley's accident until I returned several months later to take my place here at Thornthwaite Manor.'

'And you didn't think to tell the police what you saw even then?' said Skinner.

'No. I only told one person.'

'Who? Who did you tell?' asked Ovid.

'She told me, my dear,' said Mrs Bagshaw, entering the room with Hazel in tow behind her, carrying a tray with a teapot and two cups on. 'I thought you might like some tea but I don't have anywhere near enough cups. I didn't realise you had visitors. Hazel, go and fetch some more.'

MRS BAGSHAW'S CONFESSION

Hazel laid the tray down in the corner and left to get some more cups.

'I don't know why we don't have any tables in this room,' said Mrs Bagshaw.

But no one seemed interested in Mrs Bagshaw's views on the lack of furnishings in the portrait room.

'Why would our father kill your husband?' said Lorelli.

'Please don't ask me such questions,' said Mrs Bagshaw. 'Lord knows, I don't want to dwell on the past.'

'The past, of course.' Lorelli remembered the newspaper article she had seen. 'Hedley Bagshaw was a historian too. He was looking into our family history,'

'So?' said Ovid.

'That's it.' Skinner clicked his fingers. 'I bet he uncovered something in the family history that Lord Thornthwaite wanted kept secret.'

'What could he discover that was any more terrible than the truths we already know about the Thornthwaite history?' said Father Whelan.

Mrs Bagshaw looked at the floor and spoke quietly. 'I don't know what Hedley discovered but it's true, after what Nurse Griddle told me I did come to believe that Lord Thornthwaite had killed my husband.'

'Why didn't you go to the police?' said Ovid.

'The case was closed,' said Mrs Bagshaw. 'Besides, your father had the perfect alibi, didn't he? He was on honeymoon with your mother.'

'Lady Thornthwaite lied to protect him,' said Father Whelan.

'Why would you stay working for him if you believed this?' Lorelli asked Mrs Bagshaw.

'Ah, here's Hazel with the cups. About time too.'

Hazel walked across the room and placed more cups on the tea tray, but still no one poured.

'So you were pleased that our mother . . .' Lorelli paused. '. . . that she killed him.'

Mrs Bagshaw looked into Lorelli's green eyes then burst into tears. 'My poor darlings. You've grown up believing your mother killed your father. I can't imagine how that's felt, how it's affected you.'

'What are you talking about?' said Ovid.

Mrs Bagshaw let out a low moan. She looked at Father Whelan. 'May the Lord forgive me,' she wailed. She turned back to face the twins. 'Your mother never killed anyone. She loved your father and she loved you.'

Skinner laughed. 'The evidence was very clear. Lady Thornthwaite poisoned her husband. I'd stake my entire reputation as a police officer on that fact.'

'Then your reputation is worthless,' said Mrs Bagshaw, standing in between Ovid and Lorelli. 'I killed Lord Thornthwaite. I killed your father.'

'This is ridiculous,' said Skinner.

Ovid felt as though a frosty arrow had pierced his heart. 'How?' he asked. 'How did you kill him? Our mother prepared the meal that evening.'

'Exactly,' said Skinner.

'She prepared the food and gave me the night off, but I handed her the plates. I knew which was for Lord Thornthwaite. It was an impulse. I saw the bottle of poison and the plate and, in that one dreadful moment, I lined his plate with poison. I'm so sorry . . .' Mrs Bagshaw fell to her knees. She reached out her hands to the twins but they stepped away in revulsion, leaving her sobbing on the floor.

'You killed our father,' said Lorelli.

'And framed our mother,' said Ovid.

'I wasn't thinking properly.' Mrs Bagshaw's face was red and blotchy with tears. 'The pain doesn't go away when you lose someone in such terrible circumstances. You look for ways to make it go but nothing helps. Then you are told that there is someone to blame and you try to get rid of the pain by getting rid of that person...' The rest of her words were lost among her loud sobs.

'To take a life, to take that which is irreplaceable from the world, this is the most terrible sin,' yelled Father Whelan, pointing a crooked finger at Mrs Bagshaw, crumpled on the floor.

'I know. I'll pay for my sins. I deserve punishment. I will not protest when they come for me,' she said, crying.

'You deserve everything you get,' said Ovid bitterly.

'No, don't leave me,' cried Hazel, falling down by Mrs Bagshaw's side, and throwing her arms protectively around her.

NURSE GRIDDLE'S CONFESSION

'Hazel, my girl, my sweet,' said Mrs Bagshaw. 'I'm so sorry. I know I've always been strict with you but I've always loved you as though were my own.'

'I know, Mother. I know you have. Please don't leave,' said Hazel, through her tears.

Ovid and Lorelli looked at each other, both of them trying to digest the new information that Mrs Bagshaw had killed their father.

'Hazel, you'll be better off without me.' Mrs Bagshaw touched her face tenderly. 'I've never been the mother I wanted to be, the mother you deserved ...' Her words were replaced by loud heaving sobs.

'Don't say that. I love you, Mother,' said Hazel. 'I can't bear the thought of you going to prison.'

'She has committed murder,' said Father Whelan. 'No punishment is too great for such a heinous crime.'

'I don't want to lose you,' cried Hazel.

'Oh, Hazel, my beautiful girl,' said Mrs Bagshaw, her body rocking with pain.

'We'll leave Thornthwaite Manor forever,' said Hazel. 'We'll run away. We'll hide. We'll go far from here where no one will find us.'

'No, you can't leave.' To Hazel's surprise it was Nurse Griddle who burst out with these words.

'She has to leave. I have to take her away,' said Hazel.

Nurse Griddle looked down at her. 'I am talking about you,' she said.

'I'll go where she goes. She's my mother,' replied Hazel.

Nurse Griddle placed a hand on Hazel's shoulder. 'Hazel,' she said softly. The corners of her mouth curled up into an awkward smile. It was the first time that anyone in Thornthwaite Manor had ever seen Nurse Griddle smile and it made her face almost unrecognisable. 'I've wanted to say this for so long . . . too long, far too long. Hazel, I am your mother.'

Hazel turned to Nurse Griddle. 'I . . . You . . . How . . .' she began. But if she knew what the rest of the sentence was she seemed unable to speak it.

'I don't understand,' said Mrs Bagshaw.

Nurse Griddle took two steps away from her then turned back. 'I was pregnant when your father made that stupid bet that he could swim across Avernus Lake.'

'That was your husband you were talking about,' said Lorelli.

'My fiancé. We were to be married the following month,' said Nurse Griddle. 'No one knew I was pregnant. After he died, I fell into a depression. I just couldn't cope. I ran away from the village and then when Hazel was born I travelled back. I wasn't able to deal with a newborn baby so I left her on the doorstep of someone I knew would look after her.'

'All this time you said nothing,' said Mrs Bagshaw.

'How could I? I had no right. She was your daughter by then. I took this job to be near her but I knew I would have to keep my secret.'

'But the letters . . .' said Hazel.

'I always posted them from different locations so you never guessed from the postcode how near I really was. I meant everything I said. I'm sorry I gave you away. I do love you.' Nurse Griddle reached a hand out to Hazel.

Hazel stood up and walked across to the window. Outside the sun was low and the wind was picking up, bringing with it a blanket of dark clouds creeping over the blue sky.

A BEAR IN THE PICTURE

Even Father Whelan was stunned into silence by the revelations, unsure who to condemn first and for what reasons. Mrs Bagshaw and Nurse Griddle looked at each other, with tears in their eyes. Hazel refused to look at either of them. Mr Farthing looked distinctly uncomfortable. Adam felt confused. Ovid was angry. Skinner looked as though he was trying to work out how to make the situation work to his advantage. Lorelli put her arm around Hazel's shoulder.

A loud bang on the door made them all jump.

'Great,' said Adam. 'I do hope that's someone else with another dramatic revelation to make.'

A second bang rattled the door.

'Come in,' said Ovid.

A third seemed to vibrate through the floor itself.

'We said, come in,' yelled Adam.

As though in response the door swung off its hinges and flew across the room, crashing into the right side wall, knocking a portrait of Lord Elroy and his wife to the floor. Where, moments ago, the door had been, there now stood a large brown bear. It growled as though announcing itself and entered the portrait room on all fours, walking with slow deliberate steps, its head bent low.

'It's one of the devil's demons,' screamed Father Whelan, 'come to reclaim this house of sin.'

'It's no such thing,' said Nurse Griddle.

'It's the bear I met in the woods,' said Ovid.

'Hazel, get behind me,' said Mrs Bagshaw.

'We can climb through the window,' said Hazel, turning the latch and pushing the large high window but finding that a tree branch outside prevented it from opening wide enough.

'Let me do it,' said Skinner. He pushed past Hazel and tried to force the window open without success.

'Everyone stay calm,' said Ovid. 'Panicking will only make it worse.'

'Panicking? Who's panicking?' said Mr Farthing hysterically. 'After all, there's only a huge angry bear in the room with us.'

'Adam, where are you going?' said Lorelli, seeing that, while everyone else had retreated to the corner of the room, Adam was sidestepping along the wall, trying to get past the bear without it noticing him.

'I can get past it,' he said.

'Be careful, son,' said Mr Farthing.

As he spoke, the bear swung its large head to look at Adam.

Adam froze.

'Does anyone have a stick?' said Ovid, looking around for something to use.

'I must have left my bear-baiting stick at home,' said Skinner sarcastically.

The bear took a step towards Adam.

'Look at the floor!' shouted Ovid. 'Don't make eye contact.'

Shaking in fear, Adam looked down.

'What about this?' Father Whelan handed Ovid the large wooden cross that hung on a long chain from his neck.

Ovid took it and stepped forward. 'Come on, then, let's see how you like this,' he yelled, swinging the chain and bringing the cross down hard on the bear's head.

The bear growled angrily but took a couple of steps back, allowing Adam enough space to slip through the door out of the room.

'You saved his life,' said Mr Farthing.

'And angered the bear,' said Skinner.

The bear had recovered from the shock of being hit and was approaching again.

Everyone was now standing behind Ovid, who was brandishing Father Whelan's cross, trying to look as menacing as possible.

'We need something bigger to hit it with,' said Hazel.

'There's no furniture in this room,' said Skinner.

'We need to open this window,' said Nurse Griddle, who was still trying to push it open.

'Adam will come round and open it,' said Mr Farthing.

'One of the portraits,' said Lorelli. 'Use one of them.'

The only picture in reach was the one above the fireplace. In a heavy wooden frame, it was the oil painting of the twins' parents.

'No, not Ruth's picture,' said Mr Farthing, 'you can't.'

'They're our parents,' said Lorelli, 'and the living are more important than the dead.'

'Well said,' said Skinner. 'Father Whelan, help me with this.'

Ovid took another swing at the bear with the cross, but the bear had obviously decided that Ovid and his weapon didn't pose quite as much of a threat as he had initially thought.

Father Whelan and Skinner lifted the portrait off the wall. 'Move out of the way,' said Skinner.

Ovid gave the bear one more hit with the cross before stepping aside.

'Now,' said Skinner. The two men allowed the painting to tip forward so that the solid wooden frame crashed on to the bear's head, causing it to let out a howl of agony and to thrash wildly about, smashing the glass and tearing straight through the picture. As it struggled to understand what had happened and how to get free, shards of broken glass cut into its skin, drawing blood, angering the bear even more.

Everyone was so focused on this horrible spectacle that it wasn't until they heard Adam Farthing's voice behind them say, 'What are you waiting for?' that they realised the window was open.

'Quick, let's get out,' said Skinner.

'Son, I knew you'd come,' said Mr Farthing, reaching for his hand, scrambling up then tumbling clumsily through the window and landing on top of his son.

'Hurry, hurry,' said Father Whelan.

'I'll help you up, Hazel,' said Mrs Bagshaw.

'No, you go first,' said Hazel.

'No time for politeness,' said Skinner, barging past and clambering out to safety.

Hazel helped Mrs Bagshaw out, followed by Nurse Griddle. Father Whelan gave Hazel a leg up then followed her hastily, leaving only Ovid and Lorelli in the room.

The bear had finally torn its way through the picture. Wounded and confused, it had retreated to the corner of the room but, after inspecting its wounds, it was now beginning to growl angrily. It showed its teeth and moved towards the twins.

'You go first,' said Ovid, swinging the cross threateningly at the bear.

'We'll go together,' said Lorelli, taking his hand.

Ovid let go of the chain and the cross whacked the bear on the nose. The bear snarled but before it could retaliate Lorelli and Ovid quickly climbed up to the windowsill and jumped out.

A LAWNMOWER AND A BOTTLE OF CHLOROFORM

Because of its remote position, Thornthwaite Manor didn't get many passers-by so there was no one to witness the odd collection of people jumping out of the high window. And there was no one, apart from those people, to witness the appearance of a large brown bear at the same window.

'Save yourselves!' shouted Father Whelan, running away as fast as he could, his black robes flapping behind him.

'Wait for me,' shouted Skinner, following him without a moment's thought for those he was leaving behind.

The bear tried to get a grip on the windowsill to heave itself through but slipped and banged its chin, causing it to roar loudly in pain.

'Come on, son, we need to leave,' Mr Farthing said, trying to help Adam up from where he was sat on the ground.

Adam batted his father's hand away but as he stood up he cried out and fell back down. 'My foot,' he moaned. 'You hurt it when you landed on me, you big idiot.'

'Your foot will be the least of your troubles if we don't get out of here,' said Mr Farthing, tugging at his son's arm.

'Let me help.' Nurse Griddle took Adam's other arm. She turned to Hazel and said in a commanding voice, 'Hazel, take Mrs Bagshaw to safety.' To Ovid and Lorelli she said, 'You two as well.'

Nurse Griddle, Adam and Mr Farthing made their escape as quickly as Adam's leg would allow. Hazel and Mrs Bagshaw went around the other side of the house. Ovid and Lorelli were about to follow the others when Lorelli noticed someone coming. 'Look, it's Tom,' she said.

Ovid turned to see a red lawnmower driving towards them. By this time the bear had found a grip and was now climbing out of the window. Once outside the great beast reared up, let out a disgruntled roar and came at them. Ovid and Lorelli turned and ran towards Tom and the lawnmower.

'Jump on,' said Tom, stopping the mower in front of them.

Ovid got on after Lorelli, asking, 'Will this thing outrun the bear?'

'Who said anything about running?' replied Tom, pushing his foot on the accelerator and driving full speed towards the bear. 'Hold the steering wheel,' Tom said, reaching down to pick up a bottle that had been by his feet. 'I've got one chance to get this right so hold it steady.'

Lorelli held the steering wheel as steadily as she could but it was tricky on the uneven ground.

'What is it?' said Ovid, looking at the bottle of clear liquid that Tom was holding.

'Chloroform. It'll knock old Paddington right out without doing him too much harm ... as long as I don't miss. Now, Lorelli, when I say, turn the wheel so that we don't crash into him. We have to wait until the last minute otherwise he'll change direction too.'

Ovid held on tight to the side of the lawnmower. Lorelli tried to keep the steering wheel steady and Tom aimed the bottle.

'Now!' he shouted. Lorelli swerved to the right. Tom threw the bottle, then grabbed hold of the steering wheel and took control of the lawnmower.

'You got it.' Ovid looked back over his shoulder.

Tom slowed down and brought the mower around.

'It's still standing,' said Lorelli.

'Wait for it,' said Tom.

The bear raised itself on to its hind legs and let out a pained and confused roar before slumping to the ground, unconscious.

A NUMBER OF QUESTIONS

'Why were you carrying around a bottle of chloroform, Tom?' asked Ovid.

'I spotted our friend Paddington in the woods, this morning.' replied Tom, crouching down to look at the bear. 'I've been carrying the chloroform since and trying to find him. I should have guessed he would come to the house. He's probably hungry, poor chap. I saw the others run off before you. Throwing a party, were you?'

'Not exactly,' said Ovid. 'Mrs Bagshaw confessed to killing our father.'

Tom considered this before saying, 'That must have been a relief to hear.'

'A relief?' said Lorelli. 'Why would finding out that someone you've lived with all your life killed your father be a relief?'

'Because it means that your mother didn't kill him,' replied Tom matter-of-factly.

This silenced the twins. Mrs Bagshaw's confession had made them feel a range of emotions but Tom was right, having spent all their lives wanting to know why their mother had killed their father it was a relief to discover that, whatever the truth was about their father and Hedley Bagshaw, their mother was innocent.

'Did you know that Nurse Griddle was Hazel's mother?' asked Ovid.

'I'd be lying if I said it hadn't occurred to me,' said Tom.

'Why?'

'I remember when Nurse Griddle's fella drowned and she left the village. It wasn't too much later that the baby turned up on Mrs Bagshaw's step, same night her husband died . . .'

'But you never said anything?' asked Ovid.

'None of my business, is it?'

'What about us? Are we none of your business?' said Lorelli, finally coming to the question that had been hanging over both twins since finding the servants' names in the will. 'Why have you never tried to stop us attempting to kill each other?'

Tom stood up and walked to the lawnmower. He picked up a heavy chain that had been resting on the back and carried it over to the bear. 'You're a smart pair. I always figured that if you really wanted to kill each other you'd have managed it by now.'

'So you just stood by and did nothing?' said Ovid.

'It's like with plants,' said Tom. 'You get a couple of new saplings and you can water them and tend them and prune them all you like, but in the end they're either survivors or they're not. You two are survivors.'

There were still plenty of questions that the twins wanted to ask but they were all pushed aside by the appearance of Mr Crutcher and a new question.

'Why has Alfred got a gun?' asked Ovid.

Mr Crutcher was walking from the house, holding the barrel of a shotgun in his left hand with the butt nestled into the crook of his right arm.

'Stand aside please, young master and mistress,' he said.

Ovid and Lorelli did as he said but Tom moved to a position between him and the bear. 'Don't you dare,' he said.

'Now, Tom, we can't have dangerous beasts roaming around the place, can we?'

'You put a bullet in this bear, it's going through me first,' said Tom, standing in front of the bear.

'Then what do you propose?' said Mr Crutcher. 'That we keep it in the stables with the horses?'

Tom said, 'I'm going to tie him up then I'll find someone to take him away, but I will not let you harm him, Alfred.'

'It's not the bear's fault,' said Lorelli, taking her place by Tom's side.

Mr Crutcher lowered his gun. 'Very well,' he said. 'Now, young master and mistress, please come in before you get drenched.'

Lorelli began to say that it wasn't raining when she felt a large droplet land on her head. Then another. And another. With all the excitement neither of them had noticed how dark the sky had grown and that the heavy rainclouds were beginning to break.

'You go ahead,' said Tom, lifting the bear's head and tying the chain around its neck. 'Get out of the rain now.'

By the time Lorelli and Ovid reached the entrance to Thornthwaite Manor the rain was coming down hard.

'You must be hungry. Dinner shouldn't be long. I'll let you know when it's ready,' said Mr Crutcher.

'Thank you, Alfred,' said Ovid.

Mr Crutcher left Ovid and Lorelli standing in the hallway. Without a word between them the twins walked to the portrait room and pushed the door open. They surveyed the damage. The picture of their parents lay in tatters on the floor. Lorelli picked up a scrap of canvas with their father's green eyes on it. 'I wish they were still here,' she said.

'I know,' said Ovid. 'But they're not. They never will be. No matter who killed our father, it doesn't change the fact that he's dead.'

'Do you think Mrs Bagshaw will go to prison?'

'Probably. Skinner will tell the police about her confession and she'll be arrested.'

'I feel sorry for Hazel,' said Lorelli, finding another piece of the painting with Lady Thornthwaite's smile.

'At least she has Nurse Griddle now.'

'Nothing's ever going to be the same, is it?' said Lorelli.

'Perhaps that's a good thing.'

'Dinner is now served,' said Mr Crutcher from the doorway.

'Thank you Alfred. We'll take it in the drawing room,' said Ovid.

The twins went through to the drawing room, which had finally been tidied up. The bits of broken piano had been put into a neat pile. The fire had been lit, giving the room a homely feel, in contrast to the storm outside the window. Hazel entered and placed a plate of warm toast on the table with the twins' chess game on it.

'How are you, Hazel?' asked Lorelli.

'I'm well enough, thank you.'

'Won't you sit down and join us?'

'Thank you but Mrs Bagshaw wouldn't . . .' Hazel paused and smiled. 'Thank you,' she said, sitting down.

Looking into Hazel's eyes, Lorelli realised for the first time that they were the colour of hazelnuts and this must have been where she got the name from. 'How is Mrs Bagshaw?' she asked.

'She can't stop crying.' Hazel met her gaze. 'You must hate her.'

'I don't know how I feel,' said Lorelli.

'I know it's not much but she never planned it,' said Hazel.

'We'll probably never know the whole truth,' said Ovid, walking across the room and picking up a handful of ivory piano keys from the pile.

'We'd like you to stay here with us,' said Lorelli, spreading butter on a piece of toast.

'Nurse Griddle wants me to go away with her. She says there are too many memories here,' said Hazel. 'I suppose my mum . . . I suppose Mrs Bagshaw will go to prison.'

Lorelli removed the lid of a small porcelain pot. The sweet smell of honey escaped from it. She spread a globule of it on toast and handed it to Hazel.

'Thank you,' said Hazel.

Lorelli did they same for herself and took a bite. 'Hold on, this isn't Tom's honey,' she said. 'Ovid, taste this.'

Ovid looked up from the table, where he had laid out the piano keys in order, making a complete octave.

'Taste it. It tastes like . . . It tastes like the honey made by the killer bees.'

Ovid tasted it. Sure enough it was sweet and spicy like the honey that had filled his bicycle tube.

'Hazel, where is this honey from?' asked Lorelli.

'I took it from the kitchen. There wasn't a label on the pot.'

Outside, lightning lit up the sky and distant thunder growled.

'I don't understand,' said Lorelli.

'I think I do,' said Ovid, who was staring at the disconnected piano keys. He pulled out a piece of a paper from his back pocket.

'What is that?' asked Lorelli.

'It's Mother's final tune.' He hummed the strange melody. 'I thought it was an incomplete composition but I don't think it's a tune at all.' Ovid grabbed a pen from the sideboard and scribbled on the piece of paper.

'What do you mean, not a tune?'

'Look.' He showed Lorelli the name of the notes he had written above the stave. 'F, D, E, A, D,' he read out. 'F dead. It's a code.'

'What does F dead mean?' asked Hazel.

'Father?' said Lorelli. 'Father dead.'

'But our mother wrote it,' said Ovid. 'Why would she refer to her husband as Father?'

'Maybe it's a message for us,' said Lorelli.

'There's more,' said Ovid. 'A, C, B, A, D.'

'A, C, B, A, D,' repeated Lorelli.

'AC bad,' said Hazel.

'AC?' said Lorelli.

'Alfred Crutcher,' said Ovid.

Another crack of thunder shook the building and the door to the drawing room slammed shut, making

Ovid, Lorelli and Hazel jump. They looked up to see Mr Crutcher standing in front of the door holding the same rifle as before. Only now it wasn't pointed at a bear. It was pointing at Hazel.

THE ENDGAME

'Alfred, what are you doing?" said Lorelli.

'A more pertinent question would be, Alfred, what have you done?' said Mr Crutcher, locking the door behind his back.

'Lower your weapon and explain yourself,' said Ovid.

'I am afraid I can only comply with one of your requests, young master. The weapon must remain but I will explain myself,' said the sallow-faced servant. 'First I would like you and your sister to sit down and continue your game of chess, please. I do feel that you are rather dragging this game out.'

Neither twin moved.

'You will notice that the gun is not pointing at you, but at young Hazel. I will have no hesitation in firing if you do not oblige me.'

'This makes no sense,' said Ovid, but seeing the barrel of the gun levelled at Hazel he sat down opposite his sister at the table.

'What's going on, Alfred?' said Lorelli. 'What does our mother's message mean?'

'AC bad, how ingenious.' Mr Crutcher smiled. 'Bad is such a tame little word for what I've done but I suppose she was limited to letters from A to G. Otherwise she might have chosen a more colourful description: usurper, traitor . . . killer.'

'Who have you killed?' said Lorelli.

'Now, young mistress, you are familiar enough with stories in which mysteries are revealed at the end to know that we can't go charging in at any point. There is a lot to explain before your short, unhappy lives end and I think you deserve a full and proper explanation, but I do request that you keep your hands on the chess pieces otherwise I fear Hazel will not live to hear the whole of this long and, I hope, interesting, story.'

The twins did as he said, Ovid touching a pawn, Lorelli resting her hand on a rook. Outside, sheets of rain lashed against the window.

'Greed is a terrible thing. It eats away at one's soul,' began Mr Crutcher. 'That's what happened to Adam's mother. When she came to paint the portrait, Ruth Farthing looked at your parents and everything they had and she wanted it for herself.'

'We already know that Mrs Farthing was jealous of our parents,' said Lorelli.

'But you don't know how hard she worked to find a

way of acquiring some of their wealth. When she heard that Hedley Bagshaw was looking into your family history, she hoped that she might be able to find some secret that she could use to her advantage, perhaps to blackmail your father out of some of his wealth. That's why she went down to the printer's that fateful night.'

'The night Father Whelan said he saw our father,' said Ovid.

'Hedley was an excellent historian,' said Mr Crutcher. 'His research was extremely thorough. That was to be his downfall. Looking into your family he found the usual stories of villainy and betrayal that litter the Thornthwaite history, and then he uncovered a fascinating fact that was to be his undoing. He discovered that you were not, as we had all believed, the first twins born into this family. Finding your father's birth certificate, Hedley learnt that Mycroft was also born a twin. He had a brother.'

'We have an uncle?' said Ovid.

'Lord Silas, your grandfather, was a cruel man and your grandmother, Agnes, knew he was expecting one child, in keeping with tradition, so when she gave birth to twins, she panicked and, in that moment, gave the second child to the midwife, who took him away and raised him as her own.'

'And you knew this?' said Ovid.

'No one knew. Not me, not your father, not your

grandfather. Agnes took the secret to the grave with her. It wasn't until Hedley uncovered it that anyone knew of his existence.'

'Where was he living?' asked Lorelli.

'Not far, as I understand it. Still in Hexford, in a town twenty miles away, I believe. When Hedley tracked him down using the midwife's name, he knew at once he had found the right person. He was, it turns out, an identical twin. He looked exactly like your father, except for one thing.'

'The scar,' said Ovid.

'Precisely. A prominent scar on the bridge of his nose, from when he fell off his bike as a child,' said Mr Crutcher. 'It was noticeable up close, but not from the distance that Father Whelan saw your uncle leave the printer's that night.'

'So it wasn't our father he saw,' said Lorelli, glancing at Hazel, who was standing motionless, staring fearfully at the barrel of the gun.

'Hedley had brought your father's long-lost brother to the village to take his photo. He went down to the printer's to halt the print run so that he could reveal his existence in an article in the next edition of the newspaper.'

'What about Adam's mum?' said Lorelli. 'She was there too.'

'Ruth Farthing arrived to speak to Hedley, in the hope that he would have some useful information.

She got more than she bargained for when she saw your uncle. She instantly saw the potential for much more than a newspaper story. She tried to persuade Hedley to use this man in order to get her hands on some of the wealth she so desperately desired, but Hedley Bagshaw was an honest man. They fought, Hedley slipped. I wasn't there myself but I believed Ruth when she said that she never meant for him to fall into the printing press and die, but fall and die he did.'

'Mrs Farthing killed Hedley Bagshaw,' said Lorelli.

'This was the first act of murder in our story, albeit an accidental one,' replied Mr Crutcher, glancing outside to where a strong wind was shaking the trees. It whistled down the chimney and rattled the door. Lightning flashed and Mr Crutcher counted out loud.

'One, two, three, four, five, six, seven, eight, nine.'

Thunder rumbled in the distance.

'The storm is nine miles south but the wind blows north,' he said.

'What did Mrs Farthing do with our uncle?' asked Ovid.

'When Mrs Bagshaw moved to the manor shortly after her husband's death, Ruth Farthing hid your uncle in Bagshaw's End. She convinced him that he had been tricked out of his birthright by his greedy brother. She told him that the only way to get even was to trick himself back into it. She told him she could help him. Frederick had grown up poor and bitter, so Ruth's poisonous words worked like black magic on him.'

'Frederick?' said Lorelli.

'That was his name: Frederick Thornthwaite. Over the following months, Ruth Farthing taught him how to act, speak, even walk and eat like your father in preparation to take his place.'

'Take his place?' said Ovid.

'On the night after your birth your father went to dinner with his old friend, Doctor Scragg. That's when they did it. Your father visited the toilet, unaware of what was awaiting him. Ruth knocked him out and Frederick took his place. I drove Mycroft to the meal that night. I drove Frederick back.'

'Did you know what they had done?' asked Lorelli.

Mr Crutcher smiled. 'You've exposed an omission in my story, young mistress. How careless of me. I missed out the part where I went to Bagshaw's End to pick up some of Mrs Bagshaw's pots and pans. It's the part where I stumbled upon Frederick and Ruth and decided to join them in their scheme.'

'You betrayed our father?' Ovid gripped the chess piece in his palm.

Outside, the lightning flashed.

'One, two, three, four, five, six,' counted Mr Crutcher.

Thunder rumbled.

'It's getting nearer,' he said.

'You betrayed our father,' said Lorelli.

'I have always loved expensive things,' Mr Crutcher continued. 'When I took this job I thought that working at this magnificent manor was enough but I discovered that it wasn't. Not nearly enough. Ruth's scheme was the opportunity to finally get my hands on some of your family's wealth and I seized the chance. Once Frederick was in place he would distribute the wealth between the three of us.'

'That's terrible,' said Lorelli.

'Is it?' said Mr Crutcher, showing a flash of anger in his eyes. 'You think you deserve these riches by virtue of your surname? You think your ancestors became this rich by playing fair? Did my history lessons teach you nothing? The Thornthwaites have acquired and retained their money through thievery, exploitation and deception. Our plan was no different.'

'Surely our mother noticed that it wasn't her husband who returned from the restaurant?' said Lorelli.

'Yes, she certainly noticed that your father had changed that night but she would never have expected that he was a different person altogether. She was preoccupied with her two new babies. At that point everything should have been simple. Ruth was supposed to kill your father. It was the perfect crime, killing a man who the world believed was alive and well. But as you know, from personal experience, murder isn't always so easy. Ruth Farthing was weaker than she knew. She became racked with guilt, about what she had done to your mother, to you and, of course, to Hedley Bagshaw. It was at this point that she told your mother the truth.'

'She told our mother?' sad Lorelli.

'Yes, but your mother made the mistake of confronting Frederick, admitting that she knew who he was. Frederick threatened to harm her darling children if she went to the police. Your mother was intelligent enough to keep quiet about Mycroft being alive. At the time, you see, Frederick and I believed that Ruth had kept her promise and killed your father. So unbeknown to us, Ruth began to take messages between the two of them.'

'The music,' said Ovid.

'The music was a coded message written by your mother for your father, delivered by Ruth Farthing. She used library books to avoid getting discovered by Frederick or myself.'

'So why didn't Mrs Farthing release our father and go to the police?' said Lorelli.

'Because Ruth had a family too. Her husband knew nothing of his wife's devilry. She didn't want to drag them into the terrible mess she had created. She was getting increasingly upset by the thought of what she had done; plagued by nightmares, haunted by the memory of Hedley's screams. Not everyone is suited to murder.'

'F dead,' said Ovid. 'F stands for Frederick.'

'Yes, your mother's final message. What a shame Ruth took her own life before she could deliver it.'

'So Mrs Bagshaw killed our uncle, not our father,' said Lorelli.

Mr Crutcher smiled. 'Frederick was failing to make good on his promises. He was enjoying his new life and becoming reluctant to share his wealth. That's when I decided to kill him.'

Hazel, who had stood so long unspeaking, said, 'But Mrs Bagshaw confessed to it.'

Mr Crutcher's smile grew into a wicked grin. 'When I overheard Nurse Griddle telling Mrs Bagshaw what she had seen that night at the printer's, I knew I could turn the information to my advantage. I knew that with a few carefully placed words and some rather conveniently positioned poison I could manipulate a situation in which Mrs Bagshaw would take advantage and do my killing for me. Why else do you think the poison was under her nose at precisely the right moment?'

'You made her do it,' said Hazel.

'No, I merely gave her the opportunity. Manipulation is a subtle art . . . a word here, an action there, but make no mistake, Mrs Bagshaw murdered the man of her own free will.'

'So why didn't the police find out it was her?' asked Lorelli.

'I had no interest in sending Mrs Bagshaw to prison, but I was looking for a way to get rid of Lady Thornthwaite. I convinced Mrs Bagshaw to keep quiet while I led Skinner to the conclusion I wanted, that your mother was guilty of killing your father.'

'But Mother knew about you,' said Ovid.

'Yes, she did learn of my involvement. Perhaps Ruth told her that too,' said Mr Crutcher. 'If Ruth did, then it was her that sealed your mother's fate. I couldn't risk her telling Skinner. My only option was to terminate her life too.'

The storm raged outside. A bolt of lightning tore through the night sky.

'One, two, three, four,' counted Mr Crutcher. Thunder cracked loudly.

'But our mother's death was an accident,' said Lorelli.

'Thank you,' said Mr Crutcher. 'For I assume you mean that as a compliment.'

'You can't predict when lightning is going to strike,' said Ovid.

'True, but you can put the highest lightning conductor in an area where a storm is predicted. The flagpole on the central spire of Thornthwaite Manor was connected directly to the telephone and I always remember your mother saying she could never bear to leave a ringing phone unanswered,' said Mr Crutcher. 'I arranged for someone to call at the appropriate time but, of course, even with my weather predicting skills lightning is unpredictable. Had it failed to work I had a back-up plan. Happily the police never had cause to check the poisoned sherry, but rest assured if they had, the evidence would have led to Mrs Bagshaw.'

'You murdered our mother,' said Ovid.

'So why didn't you just kill us too? We were only defenceless babies,' said Lorelli.

'Believe me, I did consider it, but I couldn't afford to draw suspicion with any more deaths straight away. I decided to leave it a few years before finding fitting ways for you to die. But as you grew older I came up with another plan. You've gathered by now I prefer to get others to do my dirty work. I decided to try a social experiment. I created a suitably sombre environment for you to grow up in, one with no outside influences, one where you were taught to mistrust each other from the moment you could speak. Then, with a couple of near misses I planted the seeds of murder in your fertile infant minds. You have never been able to remember who committed the first act of attempted murder because it was me. The working guillotine, the exploding lollipop, they were all I had to do to set you off on your destructive paths. Then I could sit back and watch as the two of you tried to rid the world of each other.'

'But we've stopped now,' said Ovid.

'Exactly. You stopped trying to kill each other, so I had to start again. The attack with the bees was supposed for Lorelli. How was I to know you would let Adam ride your horse? That and the booby-trapped tree were designed to make you think your brother was back to his usual tricks.'

'And the bear?' asked Ovid.

'Lorelli had the application form to buy the bear from the closing down zoo but it was I who filled it out and sent it off.'

'It was all you,' said Lorelli.

'Indeed. It was all so you would end your truce and get you back to work, trying to kill each other.'

'But you were in favour of changing the will,' said Lorelli.

'Of course, that way only one of you would have to die for me to get the inheritance. Then, I would call the police and have the remaining twin imprisoned for murder.'

'They were all your designs I saw at Bagshaw's End,' said Lorelli.

Mr Crutcher nodded. 'And if you had looked more carefully you would have seen one involving a metallic chessboard and a lightning conductor. What a strange fate it will be when both Thornthwaite twins go the same way as their mother. What irony. The lightning is almost above us now and when it strikes it will shoot through the house, through this endless chess game and fry the two of you. Then finally the Thornthwaite inheritance will be mine. Checkmate, young master and mistress, checkmate.'

THE FINAL MOVES

As the twins gripped their chess pieces they were in no doubt that if they were to move away from the chessboard Mr Crutcher would pull the trigger and kill Hazel.

'You haven't said what happened to our father,' pointed out Lorelli.

'Ah yes, Lord Mycroft Thornthwaite,' said Mr Crutcher. 'When Ruth told me, she hadn't killed him I ordered her to finish the job. I told her to keep it simple, to take him from Bagshaw's End where he was held captive, up Devil's Leap and push him off, otherwise everything we had done would be for nothing. She tied him up and blindfolded him then drove him up to Devil's Leap, but in truth I don't believe she ever intended on going through with it. She had already decided to take her own life.'

'So our father survived?' said Ovid.

'Please don't expect this story to be one with a

happy ending, young master,' said Mr Crutcher. 'I knew I couldn't trust Ruth. I followed her up to Devil's Leap. When I saw her jump, I revealed myself. Your father was understandably pleased to see his loyal servant. He had been through a terrible ordeal.'

'You are evil,' said Lorelli.

'No, an evil man would have told your father that his wife was dead and that his children would soon follow her. I allowed your father a moment of hope and relief before I pushed him off the cliff. I'm not evil. I'm just greedy.'

'You're a wicked man, Mr Crutcher,' said Hazel, walking slowly over to the chessboard.

'Stay still,' said Mr Crutcher, his finger twitching on the trigger.

Another flash of lightning illuminated the world outside the window.

'One, two, three,' counted Mr Crutcher. The sound of thunder reverberated. 'It's almost time.'

'No,' said Hazel, stretching out her arm and sweeping the chess pieces off the board, knocking away the twins' hands.

'You silly girl,' snarled Mr Crutcher.

'Hazel, no!' Lorelli grabbed her and dragged her to the ground as Mr Crutcher pulled the trigger.

The gun made an ear-shattering BANG that was followed by the tinkle of broken glass. Lorelli looked up to see that the bullet had shattered the window. A strong wind blew into the room, causing the black curtains to flap violently.

Before Mr Crutcher could take aim again, Ovid was in front of him, holding the barrel in one hand and the butt in the other, grappling to take it off the wiry servant.

'Let me finish this,' said Mr Crutcher.

'You murdered our parents,' said Ovid. 'You would have turned us into murderers too.'

'You were born murderers. You're Thornthwaites. It's in your blood.' As he said this, Mr Crutcher kicked Ovid's bad ankle, causing him to howl in pain and fall to the ground. Mr Crutcher had his back to the window now and the curtain flapped behind him like black wings. He levelled the gun at Ovid. 'I wanted to make this neat, but if you will insist on making it messy . . .'

'Shoot me and they'll send you to prison,' said Ovid. 'You'll get nothing.'

'No. I'll blame Mrs Bagshaw.' Mr Crutcher smiled at the thought. 'I'll say that after confessing to killing your father she then found the gun and killed you . . .' He paused then added, 'before turning the gun on herself.'

'No,' said Hazel, jumping to her feet and shoving Mr Crutcher's chest.

He staggered back and the gun went off, hitting the curtain rail, bringing it down on to his head, knocking him on to the chessboard.

What happened next would haunt Ovid, Lorelli and Hazel for the rest of their lives and become the subject of countless nightmares.

Lightning struck and thunder sounded simultaneously. Mr Crutcher let out a strange animalistic howl. The noise died away and the lights went out.

Ovid got to his feet and found his sister's hand. She reached for Hazel and the three of them stood, trembling in the gloomy room. In front of them, Mr Crutcher's body lay still on the chessboard, his face horribly contorted with pain.

'He's dead,' said Ovid.

'Yes,' said Lorelli.

'It's my fault,' said Hazel.

'No,' said Ovid. 'He killed himself.'

Who knows how long they would have stood there had it not been for a new danger in the corner of the room? The derailed curtain had blown into the fireplace and caught on fire. Fanned by the wind, eager flames licked the walls, spreading across the room. The fire alarm sounded.

'We need to get out,' said Lorelli.

'We can't leave him here.' Hazel pointed to Mr Crutcher's body.

'Yes, we can,' said Ovid.

'No we can't,' said Hazel.

'She's right,' said Lorelli. 'Even the dead need caring for.'

The door opened and Tom Paine entered the room. 'Come on, it's time to get out,' he said.

'Alfred's dead,' said Lorelli.

Tom surveyed the room. 'I'll bring the body,' he said, 'now please, hurry up and get out.'

FIRE AND RAIN

Outside in the dark, the rain was easing off but the wind was still blowing bitterly. Ovid, Lorelli and Hazel were joined by Mrs Bagshaw, Nurse Griddle and Adam Farthing.

Seeing Hazel, Mrs Bagshaw threw her arms around her. 'What's happened, my love?' she said.

Hazel didn't reply, so Lorelli spoke. 'Alfred confessed to everything he has done,' she said. 'He killed our parents; he tried to kill us.'

Mr Farthing and Tom appeared from the building, carrying Mr Crutcher's body between them.

'Mr Crutcher. He's . . .' began Nurse Griddle.

'He's dead,' said Ovid.

'What an afternoon, what an awful day,' wailed Mrs Bagshaw.

Tom and Mr Farthing laid Mr Crutcher down on the grass.

'The fire's spreading through the building,' said Tom.

'The fire brigade are on their way,' said Mr Farthing.

The twins stepped away from the others and looked back at the manor. One by one, each window was lighting up, with a reddish glow.

'I don't care about the house,' said Ovid.

'Nor I,' said Lorelli.

'I have something else to say,' said Mr Farthing. 'It's about your mother.'

Lorelli looked up at the large lawyer, the red flames of the fire reflected in his glasses. 'What is it?'

'It wasn't a wrong number that killed her. It was me. Someone had left a note asking me to call Ruth on your number. I didn't know why but when I heard that the call had killed Lady Thornthwaite I became scared of what Ruth had got herself involved in. I lied to the police. I'm sorry.'

'It wasn't your fault. Mr Crutcher tricked you,' said Lorelli. 'He tricked us all.'

Mr Farthing let out a loud sob. 'Such a terrible waste . . .'

'What are you crying about now?' said Adam, hobbling over on his crutch.

'Your mother . . .' began Mr Farthing. 'She . . .'

'What?'

Lorelli patted Mr Farthing's hand kindly. 'He's trying to tell you that you were right, your mother didn't kill herself. Alfred killed her too. He pushed her off Devil's Leap,' she lied.

Adam stared at Lorelli for a moment before turning to Mr Farthing. Then, father and son fell into each other's arms, crying.

The twins walked away to leave them in peace. Without a word between them, Lorelli and Ovid sat down on the damp grass to watch Thornthwaite Manor burn.

A SHELL OF HOPE

By the time the firemen had finished putting out the fire, all that was left of Thornthwaite Manor was an empty shell.

Adam asked for permission to write to Lorelli. She gave it, providing that he only wrote the truth in his letters, and then Mr Farthing took his son home.

The twins didn't know what would happen next in their lives but as Tom Paine led them through the charred remains of their family home they felt full of hope.

They hoped Tom would become their new guardian.

They hoped they would be able to attend the village school.

For Nurse Griddle's sake and their own, they hoped Hazel would stay with them and travel with them every day to school.

They hoped Mrs Bagshaw wouldn't have to go to

prison.

They also hoped she would learn to cook tastier food.

They hoped that when Thornthwaite Manor was refurbished it would be painted colourfully, with brighter light bulbs, a TV, a computer and all those other things that normal people had.

Ovid hoped that he would make friends in the village and that he and his sister would never try to harm one another again.

Lorelli hoped that she might see Miss Wilde every day after school, and talk to her about books, and that one day she might sit down and write her own story. Most of all, she hoped that, unlike Franciska Töth, her life wasn't a prewritten tragedy, doomed from its first sentence, and that she and her twin brother could live happily ever after like characters in a fairy tale.

That's what they hoped for.

ABOUT THE AUTHOR

Gareth P. Jones is the author of the popular series *The Dragon Detective Agency*, also published by Bloomsbury. During the day he works as a television producer, writing books on the bus home. He lives in a flat in Forest Hill, which he shares with five guitars, two ukuleles, a mandolin and his lovely wife, Lisa. He is currently writing a new book about space.

More fantastic fiction from Bloomsbury

MISSING CATS, WAYWARD PROFESSORS, VANISHED SEA DRAGONS, STOLEN FILMS ... NO JOB IS TOO DARING FOR SCALY SLEUTH DIRK DILLY

'VILLAINY WORTHY OF FILM NOIR' *THE TIMES*

To order direct from Bloomsbury Publishing visit www.thedragondetectiveagency.com
or call 020 7440 2475

BLOOMSBURY

www.bloomsbury.com

'REMARKABLE . . . OUT OF THIS WORLD' *THE TIMES*

EXPERIENCE AN ADVENTURE LIKE NOTHING ON EARTH

To order direct from Bloomsbury Publishing visit www.bloomsbury.com/philipreeve
or call 020 7440 2475

BLOOMSBURY

www.bloomsbury.com

'Impossible not to be hooked' *Observer*

'A perfect family book' *Guardian*

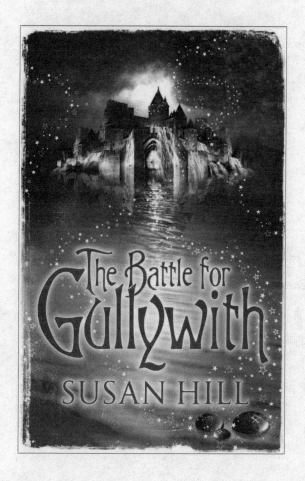

The Battle for Gullywith

SUSAN HILL

A spellbinding story of magic, myth and midnight adventure

To order direct from Bloomsbury Publishing visit www.bloomsbury.com/susanhill
or call 020 7440 2475

BLOOMSBURY

www.bloomsbury.com